MW01088071

Warlock of the Wind

Adventures in Reason

Kris Langman

Post Hoc Publishing

Warlock of the Wind
Copyright © 2019 by Kris Langman
Print Edition
Post Hoc Publishing

All rights reserved. No part of this book may be reproduced without permission of the author except for the inclusion of brief quotations in a review.

Neither the author nor Post Hoc Publishing assumes any liability with respect to loss or damage alleged to have been caused by the information in this book.

Chapter One

━━◆●◆━━

Flying Machines and Flatulence

"OH, THAT WAS an awful one, Miss," said Curio, holding his nose.

"Yes," said Nikki, her nose buried in the crook of her elbow. Her tunic kept out some of the smell, but not all of it.

"Stinker's out done hisself this time," said Curio. "I think he's going for the world record in smells."

Stinker was the name Curio had given to their stolen horse. It was a very apt name. After every mouthful of grass Stinker gave off a stench so foul that even the birds chirping in the nearby trees disappeared.

Nikki cautiously lifted her nose from her elbow, but immediately regretted it. She leaned sideways over the saddle and vomited.

"Do you want to stop, Miss?" asked Curio, pulling on the reins. "Stinker's been munching on buttercup flowers and that seems to make the smell worse."

"No, I'm okay," said Nikki, wiping her mouth. "Let's keep going. It shouldn't be long now."

The rough, grass-covered road they were riding on wound through an unpopulated forest. They hadn't seen another person for days, but several miles back they'd spotted what looked like chimney smoke rising in the sky up ahead. Dozens of narrow columns of smoke

1

floated up over the tree tops, suggesting a large village. They were both eager to arrive and beg for a place to sleep. The last several nights of sleeping outdoors on the cold ground had left them stiff, grouchy and half-frozen. Nikki almost wished they were back in ImpHaven. They'd been surrounded by knife-carrying Lurkers and sword-wielding knights, but the borrowed beds they'd slept in had been a lot softer than a pile of pine needles with a rock for a pillow.

"I think I'll walk for a while," said Nikki after another mile of holding her nose. She slid from the saddle. "If I get upwind of Stinker the smell won't be so bad." She jogged along the grassy road, trying to get out in front of the horse.

Stinker, who'd shown a strong dislike of Nikki from the moment they'd met, immediately broke into a trot. Curio pulled on the reins and yelled at the horse to stop, but Stinker just trotted faster. Curio and Stinker were soon out of sight.

Nikki sighed and increased her pace. She wasn't terribly worried about getting separated from Curio. The road was overgrown but easy to follow. And Curio would find some way to stop the horse once he reached the village. She glanced from side to side as she jogged, but saw only pine trees and the occasional rhododendron bush. If there was anything dangerous lurking among the trees there was no sign of it. The woods were silent except for the squawk of a blue jay and the slap of Nikki's worn-out Nikes.

After another few miles she slowed to a walk. The road had changed from grass to cobblestones and she could see thatched roofs and brick chimneys ahead. Small cottages began to appear on either side of the road, partially hidden by the trees. Gradually the buildings grew more numerous and closer to the road. They had sturdy pine walls and hay-thatched roofs. Above their doorways were intricate carvings of flowers and animals. Each cottage had a vegetable garden, a chicken coop, and a rabbit hutch.

The cottages soon gave way to larger stone buildings and the road ended at the town square. The cobblestoned square had a grassy area in the middle surrounded by benches where a few men sat talking and smoking pipes. Nikki entered the square cautiously, but no one seemed to pay her any attention. She approached a group of women who were washing laundry in a stone trough at the edge of the square.

"Hello," she said, trying to mimic a Realm accent. She'd been listening carefully to Gwen and Curio during the time they'd spent in ImpHaven and she thought her local accent was getting pretty good. Gwen had a more formal style of speaking, probably because she'd been brought up in a noble family, and Curio had terrible grammar, but their way of pronouncing most words was the same. "Have you seen a young boy on a horse ride by?"

The women laughed.

"Yes," said a young woman who was vigorously pounding her laundry with a wooden paddle. "He rode through here like a bouncing ball. Amazing he managed to stay in the saddle. He needs some riding lessons. Either that or a slower horse."

"Did you see which way he went?" asked Nikki.

"Down Orchard Street," said the woman, pointing with her paddle. "Toward the stables. Maybe the horse is lonely and wanted company."

The women laughed again and went back to their laundry.

Nikki headed in the direction indicated. The town was quite prosperous looking, with two-story stone buildings all around the main square. Orchard Street seemed to be its commercial center, with shops selling everything from pastries to leather goods to woolen dresses. Nikki held her breath as she passed a bakery, trying not to breath in the smell of the blackberry tarts in the window. She didn't have any money with her. She had some moldy cheese in her rucksack, provisions from their last night in ImpHaven, and she was grateful for it. But after three days of cheese a nice pastry sounded wonderful.

Orchard Street was crowded with shoppers carrying baskets and merchants trundling hand carts down the flagstone-covered street. Nikki tried to keep a low profile and was careful not to bump into anyone. That became harder as a crowd suddenly formed in the middle of the street. People had formed a circle around a man playing a violin. A tiny white dog dressed in a pink satin skirt was dancing on its hind legs, doing a surprisingly good job of staying on tempo.

Nikki stopped to watch. People were throwing coins at the violinist and bits of meat at the dog. At the end of the tune she clapped along with everyone else. The violinist had just started another tune when there was a commotion in the crowd. The circle of onlookers parted and an odd sight appeared. An old man dressed in a dirty white tunic and knee breeches rode through the gap in the crowd on a very large, very woolly sheep. The sheep was saddled and bridled like a horse and the old man rode side-saddle. He was holding the reins with one hand and calmly eating a peach with the other.

The violinist stopped playing and swept off his hat, bowing low before the old man. The crowd laughed and Nikki got the impression that the violinist was mocking the old man.

"Play on, play on," said the old man, waving at the violinist and kicking his heels into the sides of the sheep. "I have no coins for you today young jester. Dancing dogs are not a priority." He steered the sheep through the other side of the crowd and continued down Orchard Street.

Nikki took advantage of the break in the crowd and followed him. The shops began to grow fewer and shabbier. Blacksmith stalls belching smoke and sparks replaced the pastry shops. The leather-goods shops now sported saddles and bridles in their windows.

Orchard Street ended in a large stable yard. Dozens of horses were tied up at hitching posts or running in circles inside wooden corrals. Bales of hay were stacked everywhere and the air stank of horse manure.

Ahead of her Nikki saw the old man dismount and hand the reins of his woolly steed to a stable boy. The old man disappeared into a rickety barn which had so much hay sticking out from its sides that it looked like it was growing fur. Nikki looked around for Curio, but there was no sign of either him or Stinker. She wandered through the stable yard, dodging piles of horse manure. She tried to track Stinker using her nose, but there were so many pungent smells in the yard that even Stinker's trademark aroma was impossible to trace.

She was about to turn back and return to the town square when she noticed a small blonde head in the hay loft of the barn the sheep-rider had gone into. It was Curio. He was waving at her and shouting something she couldn't hear. She waved back and headed into the barn.

The sight which met her eyes made her stop in her tracks. She'd expected the usual horse stalls, hay bales, and riding tack. Instead the barn was piled to the ceiling with odd contraptions, wooden machinery and stacks of iron gears.

Pounding feet sounded in the hay loft and Curio appeared, peering down at her from a trapdoor in the ceiling. "Hello, Miss," he said. "Be right down." He jumped through the trapdoor, landing with a whoosh and a cloud of dust on a tall pile of hay covered by a canvas tarp.

"Where's Stinker?" asked Nikki as Curio picked hay out of his hair.

"He's in a corral out back," said Curio. "Mr. Warlock let me put him in there with Mortimer. Mortimer's a sheep. Mr. Warlock rides him like a horse. Never seen anything like it. You'd think a sheep would be too small to ride, but Mr. Warlock says it's very comfortable cause of all the wool."

"What is all this stuff?" asked Nikki, walking over to examine what looked like an airplane wing from the time of the Wright brothers. It had wooden ribs covered in heavy canvas and looked far too heavy to get off the ground.

"This is my life's work, young lady," said a voice behind her.

Nikki turned to see the sheep-riding old man limping toward them on crutches. He propelled himself forward on powerful arms, dragging his legs behind him.

"Flight" said the old man. "That has been my dream and my life's ambition since I was smaller than young Curio here. We have wagons for transporting us across the land, and sails for moving across the seas, but we have yet to join the birds in their joyous freedom across the sky."

"Well, there are balloons," said Nikki, thinking of the one she'd used to cross the Mystic Mountains.

The old man scoffed and waved an impatient hand. "Balloons! Toys for children. Can you steer a balloon? No. Can you dive and bank and land exactly where you intend? No."

He pulled himself over to a nearby hay bale and sat down with a sigh of relief. When he removed his crutches from under his arms Nikki could see ugly purple welts on his forearms.

The old man wagged a finger at her. "Don't you go giving me that pitying look, young lady. I get myself around just fine with the help of my sticks and with the assistance of my noble steed Mortimer. Why walk when you can ride on a fluffy blanket of wool? I'll wager the King himself has less comfort when he travels." He pulled a small contraption out of his pocket and unfolded it. It had a vertical shaft about six inches long with a pin stuck on one end. Two light pieces of wood were fixed onto the shaft by the pin. At the end of the pieces of wood were cups made out of parchment. The old man held it up and a light breeze whistling through the open door of the barn caused the cups to turn in a circle around the shaft.

"Oh!" said Nikki. "An anemometer!"

The old man dropped the contraption in surprise. "You've seen a device like this before?"

"Well, yes," said Nikki cautiously. "It's a device for measuring the speed of wind."

"What did you call it?" asked the old man. "An amomter? I've never heard that term, nor was I aware that any others in the Realm were studying the deep secrets of the wind."

"Mr. Warlock knows lots of deep secrets," said Curio, picking up the device. "That's why people here call him the Warlock."

The old man snorted. "They call me that because they're a superstitious bunch here in Border Town. It comes from being so isolated. We're out in the far reaches of the Realm. A long way from the centers of learning in Deceptionville and Kingston. Isolation and lack of education drives belief in nonsense. They call me Warlock because they think what I do is magic. Nothing could be farther from the truth. My methods involve only the careful observation of reality and the collection of verified facts. Any village idiot could do the same, but most people prefer to make up wild stories about spells and magic and invisible beings. Pure mental laziness, that's what it is. But enough about our local nitwits. I want to know where you saw another wind-measuring device, young lady. Was it in Kingston, at the house of the Prince of Physics?"

"Um, yeah, sure," said Nikki. "I think that's where I saw it."

The old man swore. "That blasted high-society courtier. It's not the first time he's beaten me to a discovery. If I had his wealth and his connections *I'd* be the leading mind in the Realm, not him."

"How does this work, Mr. Warlock?" asked Curio, holding the contraption up to the breeze and watching the cups spin slowly around.

"You count the number of turns," said the old man. "I've found that my pulse works quite well as a timekeeper." He put two fingers on his neck and watched the turning of the cups. "One turn per beat of my pulse means a slow breeze which won't even lift the heads of the daisies in the meadow. Five turns per beat means a strong wind. Good for sailing. Ten turns per beat means lock yourself in your cottage and hope the roof doesn't blow off."

"Pulse rates vary a lot," said Nikki, taking the instrument from Curio and examining it.

The old man glared at her from under bushy eyebrows. "What are you saying, young lady? That my work is inaccurate?"

"No, no," said Nikki absentmindedly, her attention focused on the wind instrument. "I wonder if you could connect this to a pendulum. A pendulum would give a more accurate count than your pulse." She'd seen pendulums in the workshop of the Prince of Physics, so she knew she wasn't introducing new technology into the Realm. "A seconds pendulum would work. One with a frequency of one-half Hertz. One-half cycle per second. If you added an axle to the top of the shaft the turning of the cups would cause the shaft to rotate. Then the rotation of the shaft could set the pendulum in motion if you got them connected correctly. You might even be able to connect a quill dipped in ink to the pendulum, so that it could record the number of turns. You could add up the quill marks to get the wind speed."

The old man stared at her for a long time, then put his crutches back on and heaved himself over to a workbench. He returned with a sheaf of parchment stuck under his arm. "Here," he said, handing the parchment to Nikki. He pulled a quill and a jar of ink out of his pocket and handed her those as well. "Draw a sketch of the instrument you have in mind and tomorrow we'll try to build it." He glanced at the stable yard outside the barn door. The shadows were lengthening and the setting sun was turning the tops of the pines red. "It's getting near dinner time. You and young Curio will stay with me. Plenty of room. You can work on your design after dinner." He propelled himself on his crutches out the barn door, not bothering to lock the door, or even close it.

Nikki and Curio looked uncertainly at each other, then Curio shrugged and followed the old man.

Nikki followed Curio. The old man seemed harmless enough. Besides, she was willing to forgive him a few faults if he was going to give them free lodging. Not to mention free food. Wariness of strangers was all well and good, but three nights of sleeping on the ground and three days of eating nothing but cheese tended to make you less picky about new acquaintances.

Chapter Two

Flying Lessons

N IKKI WAS JOLTED awake the next morning by the crowing of a
rooster. She groaned and pulled the ragged quilt over her head,
but it was no use. The rooster was giving it his all. When she sat up
she realized why it sounded so loud. The feathered alarm clock was
strutting across the attic floor right next to her bed, pecking at the
creaky wooden floorboards.

Nikki sighed and pulled on her tunic, trousers, and Nikes. After
she finished tying her shoes she spotted how the bird had gotten in.
There was a gaping hole in the attic ceiling. She hadn't seen the hole
when she went to bed because it had been dark out. Now the early
morning sun was shining through the hole, warming the barren room.
She stretched, trying to work out the kinks in her back caused by the
lumpy, straw-filled mattress. But she couldn't complain. At least she
had a room to herself and a bed to sleep in. Curio was sleeping down
in the kitchen on a mattress on the floor.

Building strange contraptions didn't appear to pay well for Mr.
Warlock, judging by the state of his small house. Half the steps of the
attic staircase were missing and the roof had so many holes it looked
like Swiss cheese. Nikki held tightly to the wobbly bannister on the
way down, ducking as a pigeon suddenly swooped in through a hole
and dive-bombed her head.

"Good morning, Miss!" said Curio through a mouthful of oatmeal when she entered the kitchen. He was sitting at a table built into a cozy nook in front of the fireplace.

Nikki took a seat opposite him. The kitchen fire felt pleasantly warm.

Curio ladled out oatmeal from a pewter pot, dumping a generous amount of honey on top. He pushed the bowl over to her. "Mr. Warlock said to have as much as you want. He's a right generous old man. Don't think he's got much to spare, but he shares as if he was King."

"Where is he?" asked Nikki, stirring the honey into her oatmeal.

"He went out at the crack of dawn," said Curio. "Said he had to get his goat into the cockpit."

Nikki dropped her spoon. "What?"

Curio shrugged. "Don't ask me, Miss. I figure a cockpit must be some kind of pit where men bet on animal fights. You know, like the goat has to fight six roosters."

Nikki just shook her head and resumed eating. She'd find out soon enough. Maybe cockpit meant something else in this world.

"Did you sleep well, Miss?" asked Curio.

Nikki nodded. "I was very comfortable, thanks."

"That's good," said Curio. "I had a lovely kip in front of the fire. Makes a nice change after sleeping on the ground. Though the bats swooped me a few times. Mice I don't mind. They tickle a little, but so long as they don't bite I can stand 'em. But bats give me the creepies. I'm not ashamed to say I hid me head under the covers when I felt 'em swoop by."

Nikki shuddered, glad she'd slept through the bats. There'd probably been plenty of them flying around the attic.

It was very pleasant, sitting in front of the fire eating oatmeal and honey, with nowhere in particular to go. But eventually Nikki felt guilt start to gnaw at her. The imps back in ImpHaven were fighting for their country and maybe even their lives. She and Curio were supposed to get to Castle Cogent as soon as possible to find allies for the imps, and here she was, dawdling.

She pushed back her chair. "We should clean up," she said, picking up her bowl.

"There's a pump out back, Miss," said Curio. "I'll show you. Also, there's an outhouse, for the necessaries. Makes a nice change from doing your business out in the woods. The last time I was occupied behind a pine tree a squirrel nearly bit me on a place I won't mention."

After cleaning up both the dishes and themselves they went in search of Mr. Warlock. There was no sign of him in the barn or in the stable yard. Finally they found a stable boy who pointed to a steep path behind the barn. The path switch-backed up a pine-covered hill until it reached the top, high above the town.

As they huffed and puffed up the hill Nikki wondered how on earth Mr. Warlock managed to make it up on his crutches. But she'd forgotten about Mortimer. When they reached the top of the hill the first thing they saw was Mortimer munching his way through a patch of grass under the pines. Mortimer gave a single loud "baa" when he saw them, then moved on to demolishing a patch of daisies.

The next thing they saw was the back end of a goat. Pillows were strapped to the goat's sides, like air bags on a crash dummy. Mr. Warlock, his crutches abandoned, was shoving on the goat with all his might. His goal seemed to be to shove the goat into a wooden container about the size of a Volkswagen Beatle. The goat did not appear thrilled with this idea. Its back feet were planted firmly and its hooves were digging trenches in the dirt.

Nikki and Curio approached cautiously, not sure whether to help the goat or Mr. Warlock.

"Hello, Mr. Warlock," said Curio. "What'cha doing?"

Mr. Warlock grunted, peering at them upside down from under

his armpit. "I'm . . . trying . . . to get . . . this . . . blasted . . . goat . . . into . . . the cockpit . . . of course."

"Oh. Okay," said Curio cheerfully. "Things might go easier if someone pulls from the front." He slipped past the goat and disappeared inside the wooden container. A sudden loud objection erupted from the goat, who apparently didn't like having its head pulled. But the pulling worked. Both the goat and Mr. Warlock suddenly fell through the doorway of the container.

Nikki poked her head inside. The container had a flat wooden floor and rounded sides, with a tall wooden shaft running vertically through its center and out the ceiling. Mr. Warlock picked himself up off the floor and tied the goat to a horizontal pole attached to the shaft. An apple dangled on a string in front of the pole. The goat lunged forward, snapping at the apple. As the goat moved the floor suddenly started turning in a circle around the vertical shaft. Mr. Warlock grabbed onto the side of the container to keep from falling.

"Whoah, Cherry Blossom!" he shouted. "Not yet!" He pulled a lever that looked like the hand brake in a car and the floor stopped turning.

Cherry Blossom gave a huffy snort and nipped Mr. Warlock on the arm. He swatted her on the nose and retrieved his crutches which were lying on the floor. "Come on you two," he said, propelling himself out of the container. "We need to get the wing tied on. The wind conditions are perfect right now."

"Perfect for what?" asked Curio.

"For flying, of course," said Mr. Warlock. He led them around the back of the container. There, lying on the grass, was a giant, canvas-covered spiral that looked a bit like a seashell.

"Oh dear," said Nikki, a sinking feeling in the pit of her stomach. She'd seen something like this before. It looked a lot like the drawings Leonardo da Vinci had done for his Aerial Screw. The Aerial Screw was called the first helicopter, though da Vinci had never actually built it, and modern aeronautical experts said it wouldn't have worked anyway, given the types of materials available in da Vinci's day. The design, intended to be built out of wood and linen, was too heavy and wouldn't have flown.

Nikki knew there were four basic components of flight: weight, lift, drag, and thrust. Weight was obvious. Too heavy and you weren't going anywhere, regardless of the other components. Lift was caused by air pressure and was largely due to wing shape and how fast a plane or other object was moving through the air. Drag was due to air resistance. A plane slowed down when flying into a headwind. Thrust was created by a plane's engine or power source. The Aerial Screw of da Vinci and Mr. Warlock's contraption both failed the weight component. They were just too heavy. They also failed the thrust component. Da Vinci's Aerial Screw had used hand-cranks operated by people as the power source, while Mr. Warlock's design apparently used goat-power. Neither goat-power nor people-power created enough thrust to lift such a heavy object into the air.

Mr. Warlock, oblivious to all the objections Nikki was mulling over, was struggling to lift the canvas-covered spiral wing. "I usually get a couple of stable boys to help me lift this darn thing," he said. "But they demand payment and my coffers are a bit empty right now."

Curio leaped forward to help and Nikki reluctantly followed. Despite her reservations she couldn't very well stand by while a ten-year-old boy and an old man on crutches struggled to lift the heavy object.

They managed to get the wing onto the top of the container by tipping it sideways. Curio climbed on top of the container and pulled while Nikki and Mr. Warlock pushed from below. When the wing was on top Nikki climbed up to join Curio and they maneuvered it onto the joint of the vertical shaft by following instructions shouted by Mr. Warlock.

As they climbed down a stiff breeze sprang up.

"Hurry!" shouted Mr. Warlock. "Perfect conditions!"

He hurried into the container and released the hand brake holding the floor still. "Okay Cherry Blossom," he said, moving the dangling apple in front of her nose, "here's a nice little snack. Go and get it!" He propelled himself out of the container and shut its door.

They moved back a few feet and watched as the spiral wing slowly began to turn. With each gust of wind it turned a little bit faster. They could hear Cherry Blossom's hooves clomping around and around inside the container.

Nikki crouched down to see if there was any daylight between the floor of the container and the ground. "It doesn't seem to be going anywhere," she said.

"Give it time," said Mr. Warlock, waving an impatient hand.

Suddenly a strong gust of wind whistled through the pines on top of the hill. It caught the spiral wing and whirled it around.

Curio's delighted shout turned immediately to a cry of alarm. Instead of lifting the container off the ground the gust of wind suddenly caught one side of the wing and the whole contraption tilted to one side.

They all rushed forward, grabbing at it in a futile attempt to bring it back to level. They heard a loud objection from Cherry Blossom as the contraption fell heavily onto one side. The spiral wing snapped off and the wooden container started to roll. It rolled along the top of the hill, nearly flattening Mortimer, who was still munching daisies. Nikki and Curio ran after it, with Mr. Warlock following on his crutches, but before they could reach it it rolled right off the top of the hill.

They could hear it crashing through the pines on the slope of the hill. When they reached the edge they were just in time to see it crash with a spectacular bang into the side of Mr. Warlock's barn. It knocked a giant hole through the side of the barn and rolled inside. A cloud of hay erupted from the loft window in the barn's upper story.

"Oh my gosh," said Curio. "Poor Cherry Blossom!"

Mr. Warlock shrugged and hopped onto Mortimer's back. "Cherry's survived worse than a little roll down the hill. She walked away without a scratch from the crash that took my legs." He kicked Mortimer in his woolly flanks. "Come on. Let's go assess the damage."

Chapter Three

———◆●◆———

Wind Power

"THIS LOOKS JUST like a hang glider," said Nikki, turning a page of parchment.

"What's a hang glider?" asked Mr. Warlock, wiping his mouth with his sleeve after a large swig of ale.

"A sort of flying glider," said Nikki, turning another page. "A flying machine that doesn't use either people power or goat power. It just glides on the wind."

Mr. Warlock was treating them to lunch at The Dancing Deer, a smoky old tavern on Orchard Street. He'd brought along a thick, leather-bound book full of his designs. They were sitting in front of a roaring fire eating bowls of stew and rye bread.

Curio tucked a piece of bread up his sleeve. "For poor Cherry Blossom," he said. "It might make her feel better."

Mr. Warlock just shook his head. "Eat your bread, boy. Mrs. Dingle will give Cherry plenty of oats after she's splinted Cherry's broken leg. That goat eats better than *I* do. She's always wandering into people's houses and stealing food from their pantries. Knows how to open just about any door in Border Town with her teeth. Mr. Tunston the baker loses at least a pie a week to Cherry. I keep telling him to lock the door to his shop, but he says it'll hurt his business. Apparently his customers are too stupid to knock on the door."

"Hmm," said Nikki, staring at a page of the old book. "Have you ever built this?" she asked Mr. Warlock, turning the book so he could see it.

"The Kite Cart? Sure. Several times," said Mr. Warlock. "I even sold a few of them. Mainly to people on the southern coast. It's very windy there, and you need a lot of wind to make the Cart go. Usually plain old horse-power works better for the farmer's carts that we have around here. Though I have driven the Kite Cart along the old forest road that leads to Castle Cogent. At certain spots the road lines up with the local wind patterns and the Cart will go like the dickens."

"Would you make us one?" asked Nikki. "We don't have any money, but maybe we could do some chores for you instead."

Curio leaned across the table to look at the book. "But Miss, if we ride this cart all the way to Castle Cogent how will Stinker keep up? It looks very fast."

"I suspect Stinker will be a lot happier staying here in the stable yard," said Nikki. "And I know my nose will be a lot happier in the Kite Cart than on Stinker's back."

"Why do you two need to get to Castle Cogent?" asked Mr. Warlock. "I was hoping you might stick around here for a while. I could use a couple of assistants at the moment. The stable boys have been upping their prices and I can't afford them anymore. I can't pay you, but I can feed you and put a roof over your heads."

Nikki shook her head. "I'm sorry, but we can't stay. We have to get to the Castle as soon as possible. And this Kite Cart seems like it might get us there faster than our horse can."

"Maybe," said Mr. Warlock doubtfully. "Depends on the winds. If you get lucky then yes, the Cart could get you from Border Town to the Castle in a day. But if the winds die then you'll be stuck on the road, going nowhere. It's just like sailing. No wind, no forward motion. Though people do sometimes keep a bellows on the Cart, just in case. It's hard work, but a bellows will keep the Cart going when there's no wind. At a very slow pace, of course."

"Have you thought about adding a jib?" asked Nikki. "And maybe a spinnaker? A jib would help with propulsion in very light winds, and a spinnaker would add speed when the wind is coming from behind the cart."

"I try to keep things simple," said Mr. Warlock. "Most of my customers don't have any sailing experience. I tried adding multiple sails to the Cart, but people kept crashing. If you don't know what you're doing the Cart is hard to control."

"I can sail," said Nikki. "I think I can control the Cart. And we really need to get to Castle Cogent as soon as possible."

Mr. Warlock shrugged. "Well, it's your neck. If you two help me repair the hole in my barn this afternoon I'll rig up a Cart for you. I have a small one already built. The local stonemason wanted it as a present for his children, but when they took it for a test ride they crashed it straight through the window of Miss Violet's dress shop. The stonemason claimed I was trying to kill his kids and demanded his money back. Mind you, I think little Tommy crashed the Cart on purpose, but I couldn't convince his doting Daddy." He finished off his mug of ale in one long gulp and belched loudly. "Come on. Let's get cracking on the repairs to my barn. That hole in the side brought down one of the support beams. I don't want the whole barn to come crashing down."

"OKAY, TRY TACKING," said Mr. Warlock. "Careful now. You don't want to overturn the Cart."

Nikki pulled in the mainsheet, adjusted the jib, and pushed the steering mechanism to starboard. The Kite Cart turned in a slow circle in the middle of Border Town's main square. Nikki swore under her breath. She was over-correcting. A tack was supposed to be ninety degrees, not three-hundred and sixty. They weren't going to get very far if she kept turning in circles.

"Try again, Miss," said Curio. "You're doing great." He was sitting on the floor of the tiny, kid-sized Cart, out of the way of the sail. The Kite Cart had a boom just like a sailboat, and it had already given Curio a nasty knock on the head.

Nikki spent the next hour doing a series of tacks and jibes until she finally felt able to control the Cart. The crowd which had gathered in the square gave her a round of applause as she stepped out of the Cart. Nikki glanced at them uneasily. She hadn't wanted to make such a public spectacle of herself, but Mr. Warlock had insisted that the square was the only open space in Border Town big enough to practice in. At least there weren't any wanted posters with her picture on them plastered on the buildings, she thought. Border Town seemed to be too remote to be up on recent events in the Realm. She and Curio hadn't attracted much attention until their Cart escapades.

"Want to try another run?" called Mr. Warlock from his perch on a nearby bench.

"Sure, but let's rig the spinnaker first," said Nikki. "I think I'm ready."

Mr. Warlock didn't look too happy with this idea, but he propelled himself over to the Cart on his crutches and helped her with the rigging. "Just remember the quick-release lever," he said. "Too strong a wind and the spinnaker'll tip the Cart right over. If you're thrown out head-first you could end up with broken bones, or worse."

Nikki nodded. "I'll be careful. Curio, why don't you wait here with Mr. Warlock while I do a test-run?"

"No thank you, Miss," said Curio stubbornly as he climbed back into the Cart. "If there's gonna be risking of necks we should both be present."

Nikki knew when she was beaten. She climbed into the Cart. "Okay, but hang on. And keep your head down." She checked the laundry hanging from a clothesline on a nearby building. The sheets were flapping strongly to the west, which meant windward was east. She used the jib to nudge the Cart into the downwind position, so that the wind was directly behind her. She gave a quick pull on the rigging of the spinnaker and it ballooned out as it caught the wind. The Cart suddenly darted forward, going faster and faster. The crowd in the square let out a collective shout as the Cart narrowly missed the statue of some long-dead mayor of Border Town. Nikki held onto the tiller for dear life as the Cart careened out of the square and bounced down the cobblestones of Orchard Street.

Nikki straightened out the Cart and was just congratulating herself on her skillful steering when the chicken suddenly appeared. Startled by the noise of the passing Cart, it launched itself out of an alleyway and hit Nikki square in the face. Nikki fell backwards and lost her grip on the tiller. The Cart swung wildly from side to side, scattering shoppers and sending a herd of sheep into a stampede. The shepherd shouted curses after the Cart, but Nikki had bigger problems than sprinting sheep. She picked herself up off the floor of the bouncing Cart and lunged for the quick-release lever.

"Aaarrgh!" she shouted. "It's stuck!"

Curio crawled up beside her. "Let me try, Miss! Maybe I can kick it loose!"

Nikki left him to it and tried frantically to untie the spinnaker rigging. She had half of it down when they hit a pothole and jerked sideways. The Cart tilted up onto its right side. It zigzagged crazily down the street on one wheel, pedestrians darting out of its way. Suddenly it overturned, sending Nikki and Curio flying.

Nikki closed her eyes, every muscle in her body clenched for an impact against the hard cobblestones of the street. But when she finally landed it was with a soft squishiness that took her completely by surprise.

"Oh my gosh, Miss," said Curio, lying on his back, half-buried in a large pile of horse manure. "I haven't smelled anything this bad since my days in Deceptionville, when I had to clean out my master's pig pen."

Nikki didn't reply. She'd gone into the manure pile head-first and was too busy spitting out lumps of fresh horse-droppings. After some very un-ladylike retching she climbed out of the pile of manure and looked around for the Cart. Its spinnaker had gotten tangled in the branches of a maple tree, and the Cart itself had crashed into a pile of lumber in front of a carpenter's shop. Its mainsail had a large rip in it, but otherwise the Cart looked like it was in one piece.

"What the heck are you two doing mucking about in me muck?" shouted a man in a dirty apron who was waving a shovel at them. "I just got this here load all gathered together. All ready to load onto me wagon, ready to sell to Farmer Nodson to fertilize his turnip fields. And here you two are, spreading it about all over the street. Now I got to gather it all up again. I've half a mind to report you two hooligans to the local Rounders. I bet a night or two in jail will keep you from this sort of mischief."

"Now Floyd," said Mr. Warlock, hobbling up to them as fast as he could on his crutches. "There's no need for that. I'm sure we can work something out between ourselves. No need to bring in the Flounders." He winked at Nikki. "They hate it when I call'em that," he whispered. "But floundering is exactly what they do. Our local constabulary isn't exactly a fount of efficiency."

The manure-seller was staring at Nikki in a way which made her nervous. It reminded her of the way the imp Tarn had stared at her in ImpHaven. As if she was a potentially valuable commodity. She wondered if there were perhaps a few of her wanted posters in Border Town after all.

"Perhaps you're right," the manure-seller said, still staring at Nikki. "It's not the local Rounders I want after all. No, I think there's someone else in town who might be more useful to talk to." With that mysterious remark he put his shovel on his shoulder and headed down a nearby alleyway.

Nikki watched him go, a worried look on her extremely dirty face, but Curio and Mr. Warlock were struggling to get the overturned Cart back up on its wheels, so she tried to forget about the manure-seller and rushed to help them.

They untangled the spinnaker from the maple tree and Mr. War-lock herded them back into the Cart, taking the tiller himself. "Come on, you two. A swim in Fern Lake is called for. You need to wash that stuff off before it sets." With a skillful hand on the mainsheet and jib line he maneuvered the Cart to the end of Orchard Street. They passed the stables and turned down a dirt road bordered on both sides by tall pines. There the wind died and the Cart came to halt.

"See?" said Mr. Warlock, climbing down from the Cart and re-trieving his crutches. "If there's no wind you ain't going nowhere. It doesn't matter now, we're only a short ways from the lake, but if you hit a patch of dead air out on the road to Castle Cogent, miles from the nearest town, it won't be a picnic."

Nikki nodded as she climbed down. She was beginning to have second thoughts about the Cart. Maybe Stinker was the lesser of two evils after all. Her deliberations ended when they turned a bend in the road and a tiny, sparkling jewel of a lake appeared, glistening in the sunshine. Nikki and Curio both broke into a run. Curio waded into the shallows with a splash. Nikki stopped to take her Nikes off, then dove in head first. The lake was deep, clear, and cold. Nikki swam to the far side and then back to Curio.

"Lovely swimming, Miss," said Curio, splashing about in the shal-lows. "You'll have to teach me, sometime."

"You can't swim?" asked Nikki in surprise as she tread water.

Curio shook his head. "No, Miss. Never learned. The river in D-ville is not the place to learn yer strokes. Very rapid current, it has. People drown there every year and I didn't want to join them."

"It's not hard," said Nikki, wading up to him. "And swimming's an important survival skill. I think you should learn. Come on, we can do a quick lesson right now. Let's start with floating on your back."

Curio didn't look entirely thrilled by this suggestion, but he dutifully leaned back, put his head on the surface of the water, and promptly sank like a stone.

"Wait!" said Nikki, jumping forward and pulling him up by his tunic. "I meant let's try floating on your back while I hold you up."

"Sorry, Miss," said Curio, spitting out water. "I thought it was sink or swim. I'm not too surprised that it was sink. Never been very fond of the water. Not since I was four, when a couple boys from the D-ville Puritanical Primary School held me head under water in a horse trough. Thought I was a goner, but me master rescued me just in time. Not that he was particular fond of me, but I couldn't do the chores if I was drowned."

Nikki didn't know how to respond to such an awful tale, which was her usual reaction to Curio's stories about his childhood in Deceptionville. Instead she demonstrated how to float.

With Nikki supporting his back and head Curio gave it another try. Eventually he overcame his nervousness, and they were just starting on the face-down deadman's float when Mr. Warlock waved at them.

"Out of the water, you two," he shouted. "Company's coming."

Nikki and Curio waded out of the lake just as a group of men came marching along the dirt road, churning up a cloud of dust. Nikki grabbed her Nikes and jammed them on her feet while the group stomped up to Mr. Warlock.

"We are taking these children into custody by order of the mayor," the group's leader bellowed.

"No need to break my eardrums Fat Freddy," said Mr. Warlock. "They can hear you all the way over in Kingston."

The face of the group's leader turned beet red. He was indeed quite chubby, with a round belly straining his military-style uniform.

"I've asked you time and again not to call me that, Warlock. It ain't respectful of my high office."

Mr. Warlock snorted. "And I've told *you* time and again, Fat Freddy, that being in the Flounders is not even close to high office."

Fat Freddy's ears turned from red to dark purple. "One of these days, Warlock, I'm gonna lock you up for good. They'll have to hold your funeral in the local jail. But I can't waste time with you now. I've more important business. These two children have to come with me. Mayor's orders."

Before Mr. Warlock had time to argue the group of men broke ranks and formed a circle around Nikki and Curio. They started marching, shoving their prisoners along in front of them.

"Don't worry," Mr. Warlock called after them. "I'll follow in the Cart. The Flounders talk a good game, but they aren't dangerous."

Nikki and Curio were marched at double-pace down the dirt road back to Border Town. They went down Orchard Street with shoppers pointing and staring. A pack of barking dogs joined them, nipping at Fat Freddy's heels. When they reached the town square they made a sharp right turn at the statue of the former mayor. Fat Freddy saluted the statue as he passed.

The men marched into an imposing stone building with tall granite columns. On its roof the King's purple flag with a golden crown in the middle was flying from a flagpole.

It was the Border Town City Hall, Nikki guessed as they passed through the front doors into an echoing lobby all covered in marble. She wasn't surprised when they headed down a long flight of marble stairs. The Deceptionville jail had also been in the basement of its City Hall. At the bottom of the stairs was a long corridor full of jail cells. Most of the cells were empty, but a few were filled with people who had obviously had too much to drink. As Nikki and Curio were locked in a cell their neighbor in the next cell started singing a tune about the mayor of Border Town. It seemed to indicate that he had dumped his wife to marry his horse.

"Old Nick Fare he loved his mare,
So much that he wanted to kiss her.
He left his wife on their wedding day
And he doesn't even miss her."

Fat Freddy ran his nightstick across the bars of the singer's cell. "Stop that caterwauling Tom Featherton. There'll be no disrespecting the mayor on my watch. Mayor Fare's the best darn mayor this town has ever had. Sure, he likes his horse. Daisy's a lovely palomino with a beautiful gait, but all the talk of the mayor kissing her on the nose is sheer slander. So you just watch your mouth or you'll be our guest in the cells for another week."

When Fat Freddy turned away Tom Featherton stuck his tongue out and waggled his fingers in his ears.

Curio giggled, earning a furious stare from Fat Freddy.

"No laughing allowed in the cells," he barked, locking Nikki and Curio's door and pocketing the key. "There, that'll hold you. Now, you two just make yourselves cozy. There's important people who want to talk to you. I'll go upstairs and see how they want to proceed." He marched his men back up the stairs, ignoring the drunken remarks floating from the cells. Most had to do with the width of his backside.

"So," said Tom Featherton, peering at Nikki and Curio through the bars separating their cells, "Do you two youngsters want to get out of here, or are you counting your blessings at such quality accommodations? Me, I come here for the free room and board, but it isn't to everyone's taste. The turnip stew they serve on Fridays has been known to cause some people digestive distress."

Nikki raised an eyebrow. "We'd like to get out of here, of course. But we're locked in."

Tom Featherton tapped the side of his long, thin nose and pulled a piece of wire out of his mouth. He hopped off his bunk and reached his thin arm through the bars of his cell, sticking the piece of wire into the lock. Ten seconds later he pushed open the door of his cell and applied his wire to the lock of Nikki and Curio's cell.

"Your freedom awaits, young lady," he said, opening their cell door with a low bow.

Nikki and Curio stared at him open-mouthed.

"Any time now," he said, tapping his foot impatiently.

Nikki and Curio darted out of the cell.

"Thanks awfully, mister," said Curio. "But won't the Flounders just pinch us again?"

Tom Featherton tapped his nose again and headed off down the corridor in the opposite direction from the stairs they'd come down.

Nikki looked at Curio and shrugged. "I guess we follow him. Unless you have any better ideas."

Curio shook his head. "Can't say that I do, Miss."

They hurried to join Tom, who was holding open a door at the end of the corridor. "Hope you don't mind leaving through the kitchens. I heard they were butchering a pig for the mayor's supper, so the floor might be a bit bloody." He froze suddenly, squinting over their heads at something behind them.

Nikki turned to look.

A man dressed in a long black cloak was striding rapidly toward them. The deep red scar on his cheek could be seen even from the end of the corridor.

"The Lurker!" Nikki gasped. "The one from Linnea's village! He must have followed us here from ImpHaven!"

"He must be the one who set the Flounders on us!" said Curio. "Run, Miss!"

Tom Featherton herded them through the door and slammed it shut, jamming a broom through the door handle. They could hear the

Lurker pounding on the door as they ran through a steamy kitchen full of pots boiling on stoves, crates of squawking chickens, and a half-butchered pig.

Nikki slipped in a pool of pig's blood and nearly went head first into a fire where a chicken was roasting on a spit. She grabbed at the cook who was turning the spit and they both went down in a tangled pile of limbs. The cook's tall hat landed in the fire and started smoking. Nikki snatched it off his head and threw it into a nearby pail of water. As she climbed to her feet she felt a rush of air as something whizzed over her head. A rope suddenly tightened around her waist. She looked up to find the Lurker holding on to the other end, reeling her in. She tried grabbing onto the cook but he shook her off and ran out of the kitchen.

"Hang on, Miss!" shouted Curio. He grabbed a cleaver from the cook butchering the pig and sawed at the rope.

The Lurker dropped the rope and lunged at him, snatching the cleaver and holding it to Curio's neck.

Nikki froze.

"Hey, there's no need for that," said Tom Featherton. "Border Town's maybe not the most elegant city in the Realm, but even our worst drunks don't go around threatening to slice the necks of children. Why don't you just put the knife down and you and me'll go have a pint at the Dirty Duck. They do a pork pie better than your own mother could make."

The Lurker ignored him and motioned with his head for Nikki to join him.

Nikki stepped out of the loop of rope and walked over to him, keeping a careful eye on the cleaver. When she was close enough he grabbed her by the hair and dragged her and Curio through the kitchen back toward the jail.

Tom Featherton followed, keeping a cautious distance.

All the cooks in the kitchen kept their eyes on their work, as if this kind of thing happened all the time and was no business of theirs.

As the Lurker dragged them through the door to the jail Nikki twisted, trying to see where the cleaver had gone to. The Lurker had one hand in her hair and the other one around Curio's neck, so the cleaver wasn't the threat it had been moments ago.

Tom Featherton seemed to have noticed this too. He suddenly sprinted toward the Lurker.

The Lurker let go of Curio and reached under his cloak.

Nikki heard the sound of a sword being unsheathed just as Tom collided with the Lurker and knocked him off balance. He let go of Nikki and staggered against the bars of a cell. Tom tackled him and they both fell into the empty cell. Tom was the first to scramble to his feet. He dashed out of the cell and slammed the door.

"Hold the door!" he shouted.

Nikki and Curio grabbed the bars of the door and held on with all their might as Tom whipped out his length of wire and managed to lock the door just as the Lurker thrust his sword at Tom's face.

They all leapt back out of sword-reach, breathing heavily.

"Oh my gosh, Miss," said Curio. "That was a close one."

Nikki nodded, not able to say anything. Her breakfast of oatmeal and honey seemed to be trying to make its way back up out of her stomach.

"Well," said Tom, "that was a bit too much excitement for me. I'm in need of a pint or three." He staggered back down the corridor.

Nikki and Curio followed him back through the kitchen and out into an alleyway behind City Hall.

"Look!" said Nikki, elbowing Curio. "It's the Kite Cart!"

The Kite Cart was parked in the alley next to a crate of cabbages.

"Should we Miss?" said Curio. "It's all rigged up."

"I think we should," said Nikki. "Though I hate to leave without saying goodbye to Mr. Warlock. We should thank him for all his help."

"I'll tell him," said Tom. "You two get out of town as quick as you can."

"What about you?" asked Nikki. "The Lurker will be really mad that you helped us escape."

Tom waved a hand. "Don't worry about me. I'll lay low for a while. Besides, I doubt that Lurker will waste any time looking for me. He seems to be after you two. What'd you do anyway? Raid the D-ville treasury? He's a D-ville man or my name's not Tom Featherton."

"Sorry, we don't have time to explain," said Nikki, pushing the Kite Cart out of the alley with Curio's help. "Please tell Mr. Warlock how grateful we are for all his help. If he wants his Kite Cart back it'll be at Castle Cogent."

Tom nodded and waved goodbye as they climbed into the Cart.

Nikki pulled in the mainsail and pushed the tiller to starboard. The Cart caught a strong breeze blowing down the street and they rolled away from the Border Town City Hall at a brisk pace.

Chapter Four

Cameras and Cupboards

"THIS IS THE way to travel, Miss," said Curio, leaning against the side of the Kite Cart while the wind blew his blond hair into a tangle. "I'm sorry we had to leave old Stinker behind. I was getting kinda fond of him despite his smells. But I gotta say, this here Cart is a wondrous contraption."

Nikki didn't reply. She was too busy straining to hold onto the ropes attached to the mainsail, the jib, and the spinnaker. The wind was whistling down the old forest road to Castle Cogent at gale-force speed. She had the tiller tucked tightly under her elbow, but the wind was jostling the Cart so much that the tiller was pounding bruises into her ribcage.

"Want me to take over for a while, Miss?" asked Curio. "Your arms must be pretty sore by now."

"No thanks. I'm okay," said Nikki through gritted teeth. The truth was she really needed a break. Her arms felt like they were being pulled out of their sockets and blisters were sprouting on her hands. But she didn't think Curio had the strength to hold the ropes, especially the spinnaker. It was pulling on its rigging with the force of a steam engine. Nikki had tried tying its rope to a hook on the side of the Cart, but the wind had shifted and nearly sent them into a tree. No, she had to be able to bring down the spinnaker at a moment's notice.

Curio twisted to look back at the road behind them. "I keep thinking I hear galloping hooves, Miss. But it's just me imagination. That old Lurker must be miles behind by now. The fastest horse in the world couldn't keep up with this here Cart."

"No, it couldn't," said Nikki. They were making very good time. She took a quick glance up at the sun. It was hovering over the tops of the pines. Late afternoon, Nikki guessed. Maybe five o'clock. If the wind held up and her arms didn't fall off they might make it to Castle Cogent before nightfall. She tried not to think too hard about what they were going to do when they got there. They had to get in to see the King somehow, but they hadn't had time to make a detailed plan.

"Curio, do you know anyone at the Castle?" Nikki asked.

"Well, there's me friend Mick," said Curio. "We was both at me master's place in D-ville for a while. Mick used to take care of the pigs. He was a couple years older than me, and he ran away after about a year. I heard that he got a job as a page in the Castle. Made a big stir among the pedestal kids in D-ville, it did. Working in the Castle's high-class stuff. Nobody could figure out how he managed it. Mick's not exactly high-class material. Bribed somebody, is my guess. He probably did a bit of pick-pocketing to get a stash of coins, then bribed a castle official."

"Do you think he'd remember you?" asked Nikki.

"Oh, sure," said Curio. "We were mates. Slept on the same floor. Washed in the same pig trough."

"Do pages ever leave the castle?" asked Nikki.

"Sure," said Curio. "They're always being sent on errands to Cogent Town. That's the village what surrounds the Castle. My master went there once and took me with him to clean his travel cloaks and shine his boots. If you're thinking maybe we could spot Mick in town, I'd say it's possible. We might have to keep watch for a few days."

"Do you think he'd help us?" asked Nikki. "Could he gets us in to see the King?"

"Hmm," said Curio. "I'm not sure, Miss. Mick was never one to stick his neck out. He might do me a small favor for old time's sake, but he's not gonna risk getting snagged by a Lurker. I'd say paying him would get us better results."

"So we just need to earn some money," said Nikki. "I guess we could do some kind of manual labor. Pick fruit or something."

"That would take a long time, Miss," said Curio. "Day workers ain't paid very well. We'd barely make enough to feed ourselves. Plus we have to be careful to stay out of sight. I'm guessing there's lots of wanted posters of you up on the walls in Cogent Town, now that Rufius is so close to the King. Might even be a few posters of me as well. Rufius the Ruffian seems to be going after anyone who's a friend to the imps."

"Yes, he is," said Nikki, adjusting the mainsail. "Well, bribing your friend seems like a good plan if we can get the money. I can't think of anything better. Sneaking into the Castle on our own would be pretty hard. Athena brought me in once using a secret entrance she knew about, but I don't think I could find it again."

THEIR LUCK HELD for the rest of the day as the wind continued to whistle down the forest road. It started to slack off just as they spotted the purple and gold flags flying from the highest towers of Castle Cogent.

"About two more miles, Miss," said Curio, peering at the flags. "And it'll be dark soon. Probably a good thing. We'll be able to sneak into Cogent Town without attracting much notice."

Nikki nodded. She hit the quick-release level on the spinnaker and it deflated like a popped balloon. The Kite Cart slowed down and Nikki steered it off the road and into the pines. It bumped along the pine needles until it finally came to a halt, its sails limp. "We'll just leave the Cart here," she said, climbing down. "It's far enough off the road that I doubt anyone will spot it."

"We should stay off the road too, Miss," said Curio as he hopped down from the Cart. "If we stay under the trees and just keep going in the same direction we was, we'll hit Cogent Town eventually."

They walked through the gloom under the trees, occasionally catching glimpses of the road through the branches. Owls started to hoot and bats swooped low over the tree tops as they reached the top of a small hill where the ground fell away and Cogent Town appeared below them, nestled in a wooded valley. The white marble of Castle Cogent shone proudly in the moonlight, perched high above the town on a rocky outcropping of granite.

"How are we going to get past the wall?" asked Nikki, frowning down at the high stone wall which surrounded the town. The old forest road they'd been travelling on ended at a gate cut through the wall, but even from a distance she could see that the gate was heavily guarded. The moonlight glittered on the guards' polished armor.

"Not to worry, Miss," said Curio. "There's a big section of the wall which fell down centuries ago. Over there, just past those trees. The Kings never bothered to re-build it. Guess they thought no one would try to get in that way, and mostly they were right. Most of the travelers to Cogent Town come along the forest road and in through the main gate. The guards at the gate are mostly for show. There's so many guards and knights up at the Castle that robbers or invaders would be crazy to try anything in Cogent Town. It's probably the safest place in the whole Realm. Well, it's safe so long as you don't have your face on any wanted posters. Follow me, Miss. We'll stay under the trees until we reach that little stream over there. If we go along its bank we can slip in through the break in the wall as easy as pie."

They scrambled down the hill and kept to the forest until the stream crossed their path. Curio pulled up a cattail reed and stuck it in the water.

"The stream's deeper than I remember it, Miss," he said. "Must have been a lot of rain lately. And the banks have washed away. The undercut's too steep to walk on. We're gonna have to wade."

"Really?" said Nikki, shivering as her breath misted in the frosty air.

"Fraid so, Miss. This is the best way into town if you don't wanna be seen. This stream runs through a tunnel under the collapsed part of the wall. The tunnel sends water to all the town wells."

Nikki rubbed her arms for warmth. "Can't we just walk through the wood until we reach the start of the tunnel?"

"No, Miss," said Curio, lowering himself into the water. "There's a big open space in front of the wall. We're nearly up to it. If we tried to cross it we'd be seen for sure. The guards patrol on top of the wall. If we walk in the stream the reeds'll hide us."

Nikki sighed and followed him into the water. It seemed to send icy shards straight into her blood. She clenched her teeth and concentrated on not slipping on the mossy rocks under her feet. As the stream left the woods the evening gloom became lighter. A sickle moon was shining overhead. Nikki glanced up at the wall. She didn't see any armored heads looking down on them. They reached the dark arch of the tunnel without incident. Curio disappeared into the darkness and as Nikki followed him the water seemed to get even colder. Her eyes tried to adjust to the dark, but she couldn't see anything at all. She stumbled along, half-swimming as she tried to keep her balance in the dark.

"You can get out of the water now, Miss," Curio whispered from up ahead. "There's a ledge along the side of the tunnel."

Nikki quickly scrambled out, but with her wet clothes and the cold night air she didn't feel much warmer. Shivering, she followed Curio through the pitch-dark tunnel, guiding herself by keeping one hand on the tunnel wall. The surface of the ledge was slick with something smelly. A rush of wings flew past her face and she stifled a shriek.

"Just a bat, Miss," said Curio. "Lots of them in here. They won't bother us. They're after the dragonflies and the mosquitos."

Nikki bumped into him. He'd stopped walking.

"Sorry, Miss. We're up to one of the side-tunnels. Just trying to remember which way to go. It's been a long time since I explored these tunnels. Mucked around in here the last time me master brought me to Cogent Town. Thought they might come in handy if I ever needed a quick escape from him. He was nasty when he drank. It was always good to have an escape route ready. I think we take this side-tunnel. If I remembers right it goes straight to a well near the granary. The granary'll be a good place to spend the night. It'll be a roof over our heads and lots of warm hay to cover ourselves with."

Nikki's teeth were chattering by the time Curio led her out of the tunnels. They climbed up a rusty iron ladder bolted to the side of the tunnel and found themselves in the middle of an empty street surrounded by warehouses.

"Storage buildings, Miss," whispered Curio. "Used by farmers to store crops they bring into town to sell at the market. Oh my stars, I'm nothing but a block of ice. Haven't been this cold since me master dumped me into a snowbank one winter back in D-ville cause I burned his dinner. We need to get warmed up before we catch our death." He looked up and down the silent street. "I've an idea, Miss. Let's head for Smithy Row. It's nearby. That's where all the black-smiths work. Their stalls should be empty by now, but sometimes a smith'll bank his coals, leaving them to burn down on their own. Dangerous practice. Good way to burn down the whole town, but it'll come in handy for us. This way."

NIKKI SIGHED WITH relief as feeling started to come back into her frozen fingers. She and Curio huddled around a pile of softly burning embers which a careless blacksmith had left in a fire pit near his anvil.

They scraped the mold off the last pieces of cheese left in their rucksacks and washed the cheese down with a jug of cider the blacksmith had left. While steam came off her wet clothes Nikki glanced around the blacksmith's stall. Scraps of iron were scattered about, anvils of different sizes lined the back wall, sledge hammers which looked too heavy to lift rested in the dirt. Wagon wheels and stacks of horseshoes indicated the main part of the blacksmith's business. "What's that?" she asked, pointing at a tall wooden box leaning against the wall. It had poles attached to both sides and was painted with shiny red lacquer and gold trim.

Curio turned to look. "Oh, that's just a Courtier's Cupboard, Miss" he said. "That what they call them here in Cogent Town. In D-ville we call them Rich Man's Rides. See those two poles? Four servants each grab an end of a pole and lift the whole box up. There's a little seat inside. The nobles and courtier types what can afford it ride around town in these boxes. Keeps their shoes out of the mud and the rain off their heads. Cogent Town is the oldest city in the Realm and it has lots of little alleyways and narrow streets where wagons and carriages won't fit. Even the King hisself uses these cupboards sometimes when he comes into town. This one looks quite fancy, with all that gold trim. Probably owned by a nobleman and brought here for repairs. Looks like the door handle has fallen off."

"Hmm," said Nikki, staring at the box. An idea about how to make some money was forming in her mind. She went over to the box and grasped the wooden carrying poles. By straining with all her might she could just lift the box off the ground.

"JUST A BIT farther, Miss," gasped Curio as he struggled to hold up his end of the Courtier's Cupboard which they were 'borrowing' from the blacksmith.

Nikki grunted. She wasn't having it much easier. They had no passenger, but the cupboard was heavy even when empty. She kept her eyes on the ground and trusted that Curio knew where he was going. She couldn't see much from under the hood of the cloak she'd found in the blacksmith's stall. The cupboard was also in disguise. They'd smeared mud all over its shiny red lacquer and gold trim. Even its owner wouldn't recognize it.

"Okay, set it down, Miss," said Curio.

Nikki gratefully dropped the poles attached to the cupboard's sides and looked around. They were in the middle of a small square surrounded by market stalls. The canvas awnings over the stalls flapped in the early morning breeze. A chicken was scratching in the dust near a pile of empty wooden crates. No one else was in sight.

"Not quite market-time, Miss," said Curio, rubbing his sore arms. "Dawn's almost here. Once the sun's up the farmers will arrive and load up their stalls with potatoes and apples and cabbages and such from their warehouses. After them the servants from the noble houses'll arrive to buy the daily shopping. We probably won't get much business out of the farmers, but we should get some good coin out of the servants. They're always ready to waste time and spend any coin they have."

Nikki nodded and opened the door to the cupboard.

Curio peered over her shoulder. "Don't quite understand the plan, Miss. Why'll people want to sit in a dark box which ain't going nowhere?"

"Because of the picture," said Nikki, clearing mud out of a small hole in the front wall of the cupboard. Just the tiniest pinhole of light shone through the hole into the cupboard. Nikki stuck her head out and squinted up at the sun which was rising over the city walls. "There isn't quite enough light yet. Once the sun's up I'll show you what our customers will see."

Curio frowned, glancing from the box to the rising sun and back. "If you say so, Miss. I'll get me stage set up." He shooed away the chicken which had wandered over to the cupboard and was pecking at its lacquered side. After dragging several empty crates in front of the cupboard he stacked them on top of each other to build a makeshift platform. He hopped up on the crates and made energetic arm gestures, as if addressing a large crowd of onlookers.

Nikki laughed as she watched him wave his thin little arms around like a politician giving a speech. She was glad Curio was handling the public speaking part of their enterprise. Her last attempt at public speaking had been during the semi-finals of the Wisconsin State High School Debate Championships, right before Fuzz and Athena had brought her to the Realm of Reason. Her attempt at a rebuttal had not gone well. She'd lost the debate and her team had not moved on to the finals. Nikki's face turned red at the memory. Memories of the debate brought up thoughts of her mother, but she firmly pushed those aside. There was no time for self-pity. A few early morning market-goers were already gathering around Curio, puzzled by what he was up to.

A rumble of wagon wheels sounded on the cobblestones and a line of farmer's carts paraded into the square. The carts split off down the rows of stalls and the farmers hopped down, tied up their horses, and began off-loading crates of vegetables and cages of squawking geese and chickens. The market stalls were soon open for business and crowds of shoppers appeared as if out of nowhere. Most made a beeline for the stalls, but a few stopped and stared up at Curio.

Curio glanced over his shoulder at Nikki.

Nikki ducked her head inside the cupboard. Perfect. She joined Curio on the platform, whispered in his ear, and hopped down again.

Curio nodded and began waving his arms like a hyperactive windmill. "Ladies and Gents. If I can have your attention. This is a day you'll never forget! A world of wonder awaits you inside this here Cupboard of Mysteries. Step right up and be amazed! Only one coin is what we're charging, though the shocking and stupendous sights inside are worth a whole bagful of coins!"

Most of the people in the crowd just laughed, though a few looked curious. Finally a woman with a straw basket on her arm stepped forward. "I'll have a look. I daresay it'll be a waste of coin, but me mistress pays me well."

Nikki jumped forward. She beckoned to the woman and opened the door of the cupboard for her. "Just have a seat inside, ma'am," she said in her best Realm accent. "And look behind you."

The woman glanced at Nikki a bit nervously, but sat down inside the cupboard as directed.

Nikki shut the door and darted to the front of the cupboard to make sure the hole was clear of mud. The morning sun had risen and it was shining directly on the hole.

A loud gasp came from inside the cupboard. The door banged open and the woman leapt out, her basket clutched in front of her like a shield.

"Sorcery!" she gasped. "The likes of which I've never seen before! Don't nobody go in there!" She threw Nikki a terrified glance and then ran off as if the dogs of hell were chasing her.

Nikki felt a pang of disappointment. Her plan had failed before it had even begun. Or so she thought, but then she noticed that an eager line was forming in front of Curio. People were waving coins at him. Apparently the idea that there was some kind of sorcery inside the cupboard was a selling point. People were eager to see it for themselves. Nikki checked that her hood was pulled down low over her face and led the next person in line into the cupboard.

What the woman with the basket had seen was an image of the marketplace shining through the hole and displaying on the back wall of the dark cupboard like a tiny movie. The hole turned the cupboard into a camera obscura, an early precursor to a modern camera. The image was displayed upside down due to the fact that light travels through the air in a straight line. So light from higher up in the sky traveled through the hole at a steeper angle and hit the wall of the cupboard lower down. The opposite happened for light lower down in the sky. So the tops of the market stalls displayed on the bottom of the image inside the cupboard, and the chickens scratching in the dirt displayed on the top of the image. Nikki knew the human eye did exactly the same thing, with light rays coming in through the cornea and hitting the retina at the back of the eye upside down. Then the brain reversed the image so that it was right-side up again.

The second customer was a large woman with smudges of flour on her cheeks and in her hair. Nikki guessed that she was a cook for one of the noble houses.

"My stars," said the cook, pressing trembling hands to her floury cheeks as she came out of the cupboard. "That's a sight to scare the horns off the devil himself! What is causing that picture young lady?"

Nikki shook her head. "Sorry, we can't reveal the ways of our magic. The spirits we commune with are very sensitive to any questioning of their powers."

The cook nodded as if this was an extremely sensible answer and staggered off.

Nikki felt guilty about misleading her, but she knew that magic and spirits were much more likely to attract customers than a rational explanation of light rays. Mr. Warlock back in Border Town would have been fascinated by what she could tell him about the physics of light, but most people, both back in Wisconsin and here in the Realm, were all too quick to believe in magic and all too slow to carefully learn the facts about the natural world. Belief in magic appealed to people's emotions, while learning physics required some tough thinking.

Two hours later Curio hopped down from his pile of crates. His audience had disappeared.

"That's all we're gonna get this morning, Miss," he said, jingling the flour sack he'd been storing the coins in. "The morning shopping's done and people have to get back to their jobs. I guess we could try our luck again tomorrow, but we've got quite a haul already. If you'll take my advice I say we return the cupboard and lay low for a bit. We're lucky that the local Rounders haven't been sniffing around. They don't take kindly to what you might call street performers here. They think it's the same as begging. And you can't bribe the Rounders here, not like you can in D-Ville. Cogent Town's kind of a stiff-necked place. Everyone thinks they have to set an example for the rest of the Realm, cause the King and his castle are here." He glanced at the cupboard. "Mind if I takes a quick peek, Miss?"

"Of course," said Nikki, holding the door open.

When Curio came out again there was a strange, thoughtful expression on his usually cheerful face. "I don't rightly understand what I saw in there, Miss. But if I had to give my opinion I'd say that your world is very different from ours. You just seem to know lots more than we do."

Nikki didn't know what to say. She hadn't yet gone into detail with Curio about where she'd come from, and after all the trouble she'd had in the Realm from Rufius, the Lurkers, Fortuna, and Avaricious she was wary of discussing her life in Wisconsin, even with Curio.

Curio looked at her gravely for a few seconds, then shrugged. "Come on, Miss. Let's get this cupboard back before it's missed."

Chapter Five

Friends in High Places

"WANT ANOTHER BLUEBERRY tart, Miss?" asked Curio.

"No, thanks. I'm full," said Nikki, brushing crumbs off her borrowed cloak.

Curio had used some of the coins they'd earned to buy hot pastries from a local bakery. Nikki sighed in contentment and leaned back against the pile of hay bales they were sitting on. They had found an out-of-way stable-yard near the blacksmith stall where they'd spent the night. A groom was whistling somewhere, and a stray dog was whining at them as if expecting his own blueberry tart, but otherwise the yard was quiet. A spot of sun warmed the hay bales. It was just right for a nap. Nikki was just shutting her eyes when Curio jumped up.

"There he is Miss! It's Mick!"

Nikki sat up and looked where he was pointing. A scrawny teenage boy in a purple-velvet page uniform had entered the stable-yard. He went up to a groom who was cleaning the hooves of a black horse. The purple and gold flag belonging to the King was tacked up on the wall of the horse's stable box. Coins changed hands and the groom led the horse out of its box. The teenage boy was just about to mount when Curio darted up to him.

"Hoy there, Mick. How's it going?"

Mick dropped the reins he was holding and took his foot out of the stirrup. He turned to Curio with a startled look. "Well, I'll be blasted! If it ain't little Curio the Curious! What're you doing in Cogent Town? Didn't think you'd ever make it out of the dregs of D-ville."

"I seen a few things since our D-ville days," said Curio. "I've even been all the way to Kingston, if you can believe it."

Mick's skeptical expression said he didn't believe it. "What can I do for ya, Curio? I'm in a bit of hurry. Have to take a message to the mayor of Popularnum." He proudly patted the bag hanging from his belt.

"Can it wait for a bit, Mick?" asked Curio. "We has urgent business up at the castle. What we need is an introduction so we can get in nice and smooth like, with no questions."

Mick shot a glance at Nikki, who was standing well back with her hood covering her face.

"Who's yer friend, Curio?" asked Mick.

Curio waved the question off. "No one, Mick. Just a fellow traveler I met on the road into town. Now, come on. What'd you say? We can pay you well fer just a few minutes of yer time." He shook the flour sack full of coins.

Mick's eyes lit up at the jingling sound. "I don't know, Curio. This here message is awful important. It'd take a lot of coins to make me delay."

Curio reached into the bag. "How about ten?" he asked, the gold-covered coins shining on his palm.

Mick snorted. "Ten won't even get you through the front gate, Curio me lad."

Curio sighed. "Fifteen?"

"Better," said Mick. "That'll get you through the gate and past the outer guard room. Course, there's still the inner one. The guards in there spend a lot of time drinking and playing cards, still, they're likely to notice a couple of strangers wandering around the castle."

Curio dug into the bag again. "Twenty and that's me final offer. We ain't paying more than that. There's others who'll help us for less."

"Done and done," said Mick. He snatched up the coins and dropped them into his message bag. He handed the reins back to the groom and gestured to Curio to follow him. He led them rapidly out of the stable-yard and through the narrow cobbled streets of Cogent Town. It was noon and the streets were mostly deserted. The townsfolk could be seen through the windows of the local taverns, quaffing ale and eating meat pies.

"Hold on there Mick," huffed Curio, trying to keep up with the longs legs of the older boy. "What exactly is yer plan here? Don't you have no instructions for us?"

"Nope," said Mick. "Just keep your mouths shut and do what I say. Don't worry. I can get you into the castle all right. No one knows its inner workings better than I do. Been studying them for years. All the secret passages and all the innermost chambers. Who to bribe, who to flatter, who to avoid. Speaking of avoiding, there's an ugly piece of nastiness up at the castle right now name of Rufius. Avoid him like the plague, Curio me lad. A walking piece of darkness, he is. Even worse than old Maleficious, if you can believe that. Maleficious was a cranky old nutter, but as long as you fluffed up his ego he'd eat outta your hand. But Rufius is a different breed of cat. Sees through ego-stroking, he does. Wants power and lots of it. That's his guiding light. Old Mally's dead, by the way, in case you didn't know. Lots of people up at the castle think Rufius poisoned him. Put something nasty in his wine, so they say. Tried to find out the truth of it myself, but Rufius is slippery. Probably no one will ever prove it."

Nikki stumbled, shocked to find out that Rufius was up at Castle Cogent. She'd thought he was still in ImpHaven.

Curio darted back to her and grabbed her arm. "Don't worry, Miss," he whispered. "It's a big castle. I'm sure we can avoid old

Ruffian."

Nikki reluctantly allowed herself to be pulled along. She didn't share Curio's lack of concern about Rufius's surprise presence up at the castle. She wondered what had happened in ImpHaven that had caused him to abandon its invasion. Had the imps somehow managed to repel the invaders? That seemed unlikely. Things hadn't been going well for the imps. But maybe they'd gotten help, perhaps from the Prince of Physics in Kingston. She was jarred out of her worries when Mick came to a sudden stop.

"All right then," said Mick. "Here we are."

They'd reached the edge of town and the steep road leading up to Castle Cogent rose before them. It was lined with slow-moving farm carts pulled by teams of horses. The carts were loaded down with live chickens and geese and baskets full of apples, potatoes, and turnips.

Mick hopped onto the back of a cart full of turnips. It was the last cart in line, and the driver didn't seem to notice that he suddenly had a passenger.

"Won't they see us when they unload the carts?" asked Curio as he climbed on.

"Nope," said Mick. "These are headed for the lower kitchens of the castle, where the pages and other servants eat. These carts won't be unloaded until tomorrow morning, and no one ever bothers to search them. Just get back there behind the baskets and you'll be safe as anything."

Nikki and Curio crawled as far back into the cart as they could, hiding behind tall baskets of turnips. The turnip greens spilled over the tops of the baskets and made a canopy over their heads. Mick sat on the back of the cart swinging his legs. They had a long slow ride as the line of carts lumbered up the hill. When they finally reached the top they heard a rumbling sound as the carts crossed the huge wooden drawbridge over the castle moat. Looking up Nikki saw the sharp spikes of the portcullis looming far above them. She could hear the guards at the gate talking quietly among themselves, but none of them seemed to pay any attention to the line of carts.

Between the high sides of the cart and the canopy of turnip greens Nikki couldn't see much, but as the cart rumbled along a gravel path she caught a glimpse of a silver fountain shaped like a leaping salmon. Water jetted from the salmon's mouth. They were in the courtyard where she'd been introduced to the King on her very first day in the Realm of Reason. It gave her an odd feeling of nostalgia. She now had actual memories of past places in the Realm, as if this was her home now. A feeling of guilt washed over her as she thought of her mother and her friends back in Wisconsin. That was her home, of course. She was just visiting the Realm, as if on a very long vacation. Not a very fun vacation, she thought with a shiver. She'd miss Fuzz, Athena, Curio, and Gwen when she went back home, but it would be really nice to sleep in her own bedroom again, and to walk down a street without having to hide her face under a hood.

The cart passed out of the salmon fountain courtyard and headed down a dark narrow tunnel with brick sides. A trickle of smelly water splashed under the wheels of the cart. They seemed to be going downhill, and when they emerged from the tunnel Nikki could see the white marble walls of the castle towering above them.

"Okay, out you get," said Mick.

Nikki and Curio crawled cautiously out from between the turnip baskets, but no one was paying the cart any attention. The driver lashed the horses to a hitching post and disappeared through a nearby doorway. They were in the middle of what looked like a small village built right onto the walls of the castle. A huge outcropping of granite jutted out from the castle hill and formed a sort of town square. The castle's kitchens and stables were clustered around it. A pen full of pigs was perched right on the edge of the granite outcropping. The pigs didn't seem to mind. They were happily rolling and grunting in the mud.

"This way," said Mick, leading them into a two-story wooden building with a brass feather nailed to the door. They entered an empty room with long wooden tables and benches. "Where us pages eats," Mick said briefly. "Everybody's out on duty right now." He headed down an unlit hallway and opened a door. "Uniform room," he said, gesturing at the rows of purple velvet coats and knee-breeches hanging from pegs on the walls. A pile of floppy velvet hats filled a straw basket, each with a jaunty yellow feather sticking out of it.

"Not the most elegant costume, I gotta admit," said Mick, "But useful. Once yer in a page's uniform nobody pays the slightest attention to you. You can go wherever you want and do whatever you want. I'll leave you to it." He went out, shutting the door behind him.

It took them a while to find clothes small enough for Curio, but eventually he settled on a pair of breeches which were a trifle too big and went out into the hallway to change. Nikki had an easier time finding something which fit. She rolled up the black trousers Kira had given her and pulled a pair of purple velvet breeches over them. She buttoned the pages coat over her tunic. It was bulky and uncomfortable, but she didn't want to leave her clothes behind. Someone might find them and start asking questions. Also she didn't want to spend the rest of her time in the Realm wandering around in purple velvet breeches. She tucked her hair up under one of the floppy hats and pulled off her Nikes, shoving them under her coat. A muddy pair of leather shoes had been discarded in a corner. They were too small, but after pulling out the laces she managed to tug them on.

"Miss, are you ready?" Curio whispered from out in the hall.

Nikki opened the door. Curio's jacket sleeves hid his hands and his breeches fell almost to his ankles. Nikki rolled up his sleeves and pant legs. He still looked like a small boy play-acting at being a page, but it would have to do. She plopped a hat on his head, which promptly fell down over his nose.

Curio stuffed the dirty shirt and pants he'd been wearing under the hat. "That should do it, Miss. I can see again. Wouldn't do to wander around the castle like a blind person. You look very page-like. Keep that hat pulled down and even old Rufius hisself won't recognize you."

They went back out to the room full of empty tables. Mick was sprawled on a bench snoring away.

Curio grabbed Mick's shoes and knocked them together. "C'mon Mick. No time for snoozing. We gots to see the King."

Mick sat up and put his hat back on, giving the yellow feather a tug so that it stuck up straight. "Slow down little Curio. We can't just go barging into the throne room. Besides, I never talked to the King in me life. Us pages don't talk to him directly. We gets our orders from the King's advisers. But I gots an idea. I think old Carmela is our best bet. She's a nice old lady. She manages the King's household. Gotta watch yerself around her, cause she likes to flirt with all the pages, but mostly she's a decent sort. Gives us extra food leftover from the King's own table. Now's a good time to go see her. She should be in her chambers working on the household accounts."

Mick disappeared for a moment and returned carrying two dusty, leather-bound books. He hand one to Nikki and one to Curio. "Us pages frequently bring account books up to Carmela. Records from all the shops in town that send goods up to the castle. Bakers, butchers, cheese mongers. These'll make you look like yer on official business. Doubt anyone'll question us, but if they do leave the talking to me. I'll tell'em yer apprentice pages, following me around cause you don't know the ropes yet."

He led them back past the uniform room and up a creaky wooden staircase which seemed to have no end. It led up a long shaft with no windows, so it was hard to tell exactly where they were going.

"How much further?" gasped Curio after the twentieth flight.

"Ten more stories," said Mick. "The Page House is a long ways down from the castle. All the pages and servants sleep down there at the lower level. The maids and grooms and footmen all have their own houses just like us pages. But they can usually catch a ride up to the castle on one of the carts. Not us though. Us pages are bottom of the heap and we gotta walk. It's an easier climb if you use the tunnels, but this here's a shortcut. Goes straight up the side of the cliff. You gets used to it."

By the time they reached the top even Mick was puffing a bit. He shoved open a heavy wooden door and waved them into a dark stone passageway that smelled like roasted chicken.

Mick took a long sniff. "Mmm. Cook's making chicken 'n gravy tonight. That's the kitchen just down there. The main kitchen's down below, next to the Page House, but they gots a kitchen up here for the finishing touches. Cause if they tried to cook everything down below it'd be cold by the time they got the food up to the dining hall."

He led them down the hall past storerooms full of barrels of ale, bottles of wine, bolts of cloth, piles of leather scraps, rows of spears and shields, shelves of parchment scrolls and leather-bound books. The floor slanted upward and as they climbed the air began to smell fresher and small windows cut into the stone walls let in beams of light.

Mick stopped at a heavy oak door painted with bright blue corn-flowers and orange tulips. "Carmela's chambers," he said, knocking.

The door was opened by a dark-haired young woman not much older than Mick. She wore a white cotton dress covered by a full-length apron.

"Hello, Annie me dear," said Mick, flashing a grin. "Is your mistress in?"

Annie rolled her eyes at him. "She's in, but I don't know if she'll want to see the likes of you, Mick the Moocher."

Curio snickered.

"Who are your friends, Mick?" asked Annie. "Never seen them before, and I thought I knew every page by sight."

"Never mind them, Annie me love," said Mick. "They're just new recruits. I'm training 'em. Not sure if we'll keep them. Kind of slow on the uptake, they are. Now, let us in old girl. We gots the accounts from Babington's Bakery what Carmela wanted. She wants to double check the figures. Seems Babington's been over-charging for his honey-glazed peach tarts."

Annie shrugged and waved them inside. "Carmela's in her office. You know the way."

The chambers were a large suite of rooms with luxurious furnishings. The chairs were all hand-carved oak with red velvet cushions. The windows had red velvet drapes which hung to the floor. Mick led them into a large, sunny, room where a very fat old woman in an ink-stained blue dress was seated at a desk.

"Carmela, me darling," exclaimed Mick, giving the old woman a kiss on the cheek. "I hopes things are well with your lovely self."

The old woman winked at him and pushed a lock of gray hair behind her ear with ink-stained fingers. "Mick, you sly trickster. Where've you been hiding yourself. Haven't seen you for days."

"Been out on the road mostly," said Mick, throwing himself into a cushy armchair. "Delivering important messages for the King. Speaking of his royal highness, these two apprentices are all agog at working here in the castle. From the provinces, they are. Never even seen a noble, much less the King. It's their fondest wish to have a glimpse of his highness. I was thinking, if you had some little errand to the King's council, maybe I could send them. Give them a real thrill, it would."

"Hmm," muttered Carmela skeptically. "That's not the kind of task I generally give to apprentices. Pages have to be on their best behavior at the King's council."

"Not to worry," said Mick. "They're very well behaved. A bit slow, maybe. And not well-educated, but very polite. So, what d'you say Carmela me love? From the outer regions of the Realm yerself you are. You remember what it was like, seeing the castle and the King hisself for the very first time. Quite a thrill it was, I'm sure."

Carmela rolled her eyes, but she laughed as she heaved herself out of her chair. She patted Mick on the cheek, leaving a smudge of ink. "Oh, all right, you sweet-talking lad. They can go to tonight's council as waiters. But if they cause any trouble it'll be on your head." She tucked an ink-stained quill behind her ear and waddled out of the office, giving Curio a pat on the head as she passed.

"Waiters?" said Nikki. "You mean we'll be serving them food?"

"Nah," said Mick. "Waiter means you wait. You stand against the wall, out of the way. And when one of the council members wants to send a message to someone in the castle or in town you takes the message."

Nikki nodded, frowning thoughtfully down at the floor. She didn't see how this was going to help them speak to the King. They couldn't very well talk to him with the whole council watching. But at least it was a start.

"Well, I'll be off," said Mick, climbing out of the cushioned chair. "I still has to deliver that message to Popularnum."

"Yer just gonna leave us here, Mick lad?" said Curio. "We paid you twenty good coins to get us to the King."

"And I have," said Mick. "You'll be right in the council room with him. Don't worry your little head, Curio the Curious. You'll be fine. Just stay in these chambers until it's time for the council. Carmela'll tell you when it's time, and she can send one of her helpers to show you the way. If you ask nice she'll even give you dinner." And with that he strolled out of the room.

Nikki and Curio stood looking at each other.

"Well, Miss," said Curio. "I guess he's right. We'll get to see the King. But seeing him won't help us much. Talking to him on his own, that's what we need. Very difficult, that'll be. He's always got advisors and courtiers hanging around him, I'm sure."

Nikki nodded. "I guess we go to this council and keep our eyes open. I've met the King twice before, so he might recognize me. But that's not a good thing if Rufius is there. He might . . ." She was interrupted by the sudden appearance of a cat. It dashed into the room and pawed at her leg.

"Oh my gosh!" Nikki exclaimed. "It's Cation!"

Curio looked down at the cat skeptically. "Are you sure Miss? Cats all look alike to me. And besides, your kitten was left with Miss Linnea way back in ImpHaven. Don't see how it could have gotten here unless cats can fly."

Nikki stooped and picked up the cat, which curled up in her arms and purred loudly. "Yes, I'm sure. She's grown a bit, but it's definitely Cation. See? She's still got that little scratch on her nose from when she got into a fight with a seagull on Griff's ship." She rushed out of the office, still holding Cation. "Where are they? They must be here."

"Who, Miss?" asked Curio.

"Athena and Fuzz. Maybe even Gwen. They must have brought Cation with them." She dashed through all the rooms in Carmela's chambers, but there was no sign of the imps.

Annie, Carmela's assistant, was sorting through a pile of parchment laid out on the dining room table.

"Where did this cat come from?" asked Nikki, holding out Cation.

Annie looked up in surprise. "Don't rightly know," she said with a shrug. "It just appeared at the outer door one day. Carmela kept it cause we needed a mouser anyway. The little varmints were everywhere. Let me tell you, it's not nice waking up in the morning to find a mouse napping on your forehead. This here cat's been doing her duty quite smartly. Haven't seen a whisker of a mouse in more'n a week."

Nikki looked from Annie to Cation to Curio. "But they *must* be here," she said.

"Who?" asked Annie.

"Nobody, Miss," said Curio, tugging on Nikki's page jacket. "Sorry to bother you." He pulled Nikki back into Carmela's empty office, where she collapsed into the chair Mick had been sitting in.

"They *have* to be here," she insisted, cradling Cation in her arms. The idea that Athena and Fuzz were in the castle was wonderful. Not just because they were her friends, but because it meant they could take over. They could talk to the King, and handle Rufius, and all the weight of responsibility she'd been carrying since ImpHaven would lift from her shoulders. Her eyes started to well up and she gave herself a vicious pinch on the arm to stop herself from crying.

Curio patted her on the shoulder. "They might be here, Miss. They might indeed. Don't see how the cat could've gotten here otherwise. But we can't run around asking people if they've seen the King's emissaries. I'm sure Miss Athena and Mr. Fuzz are staying outta sight if they're here. Rufius will throw them straight into the castle dungeon if he spots 'em. He'll be able to do it without the King even knowing about it. You know how sneaky he is."

"I know," said Nikki. "I'll be more careful." She scratched Cation under the chin. "If Fuzz and Athena *are* here I wonder what it means. Maybe they managed to fight off the Knights of the Iron Fist and ImpHaven is saved."

Curio looked at her with both eyebrows raised.

Nikki sighed. "Yeah, you're right. I don't see how the imps could possibly have fought off the Knights." She stood up and tucked Cation on her shoulder. The kitten was a long-legged teenager now, but she managed to stay on her perch by sticking her claws into Nikki's velvet page jacket. "C'mon," said Nikki. "Let's go see if we can scrounge some food."

Chapter Six

Enemies in High Places

NIKKI TRIED DESPERATELY not to scratch her nose. She had her page's hat pulled down low over her face and its feather was tickling her nostrils. It itched like crazy, but she didn't want to draw even the slightest attention to herself. She'd left Cation out in the hall and she and Curio had plastered themselves against the wall of the King's council chamber, standing in the shadow of a large marble statue of Maleficious, the King's very unpleasant and very deceased advisor. The statue showed him smiling, which was something Nikki doubted he'd ever done when he was alive. She took a deep breath and tried not to think about her nose. So far the council had gone better than she'd expected. For one thing, Rufius wasn't there. It was just the King and a small group of his advisors sitting around a table drinking ale and eating a roast chicken which Carmela had brought in. It seemed to be a very informal council, thought Nikki. She'd expected a much larger group, with people giving speeches and begging the King for favors. So far no one had asked for any messages to be sent anywhere. She and Curio could be marble statues themselves for all the attention anyone paid to them.

The council went on for about an hour with nothing interesting happening. Beside her she heard Curio yawn as the talk shifted from taxes on imports of silk from the Southern Isles to taxes on wheat and barley crops. Nikki was stifling a yawn herself when the council door suddenly banged open.

The King spilled his ale and two of the council members jumped to their feet. A large group of rough-looking men surged into the room. Nikki gasped as she recognized their leader. There was no mistaking that empty eye socket with the knife scar running down the middle of it. It was the man from the Mystic Mountains. The leader of the strange group who lived in isolation on a mountain top and who worshipped Maleficious. She'd forgotten all about them during the desperate situation of the imps and the attempt to save ImpHaven.

Nikki glanced nervously from their leader to the King. The leader's vow to revenge the death of Maleficious came back to her. He'd somehow gotten the idea that the King was responsible.

All of the King's council members were now on their feet and standing in front of the King, but they were outnumbered three to one by the men of the Mystic Mountains. Nikki began sliding along the wall towards the door to go get help, when to her relief a troop of castle guards armed with spears marched into the room. They surrounded the Mystic men, not quite pointing their spears at them, but hinting very strongly that they'd like to.

The King stepped forward, motioning to the guards to lower their spears.

"Citizens," he said, wiping some spilled ale off his midnight-blue tunic and adjusting his crooked crown, "you are interrupting a private council. But I forgive you. Clearly you have some urgent business which allows no time for manners. Please state your business."

The leader of the Mystic men slowly pointed to the statue of Maleficious.

The King and his council members looked at the statue in bafflement. Nikki and Curio slid along the wall away from it.

"I'm afraid I don't follow you," said the King. "Granted, it's a skillful piece of artwork. We have a new sculptor here at the castle.

He's a wizard with marble. He did a lovely little piece for my chambers. A fawn smelling daffodils. I smile every time I look at it."

The remaining eye of the leader of the Mystic men bulged in fury. "We are here to avenge him," he rasped.

"Avenge who?" asked the King. "The fawn? I don't think any fawns were actually harmed during the sculpting process."

The vein in the leader's empty eye-socket started to pulse. "We are here to avenge the death of Maleficious."

The King's mouth dropped open in surprise. "My dear fellow," he said. "There's nothing to avenge. Poor old Mally died of entirely natural causes. He was getting on in years, you know. Old age eventually catches up with all of us."

At that moment a young man dressed in a spotless black tunic and sandals sauntered into the room.

Curio elbowed Nikki and whispered "Poofius" under his breath.

Rufius strolled through the ring of spears as if taking a walk in the King's rose garden. He perched on the edge of the table and poured himself a tankard of ale. "Actually," he said, "I believe the healers in the castle were a trifle concerned about the health of Maleficious right before the end. He'd been having some stomach problems. I believe the word 'poison' was even mentioned."

The face of the leader of the Mystic men turned beet red, but the King waved an impatient hand.

"Nonsense," said the King. "Mally was always having stomach problems. He had indigestion even as a young man when he served during my father's reign. It was a life-long health issue. There was no foul play whatsoever. We all have these little health problems. I myself have the most dreadful allergy to bees. Not bee stings, just bees. I sneeze my head off if a bee so much as flies past my nose."

Rufius shrugged and took a sip of ale. "Well, since my esteemed master, the late Maleficious, is dead and buried we'll never know the real truth of the matter. If I may make a suggestion, your Highness, why don't you let me deal with these men. I'll take them down to the guesthouses on the lower level and discuss their concerns with them. I'm sure I can straighten this matter out." He turned his head slightly and winked at the leader of the Mystic men.

Nikki saw the wink and had to bite her tongue to keep from gasping. Rufius and the Mystic men knew each other.

The King had not seen the wink. He gave a sigh of relief and patted Rufius on the back. "Excellent! That is a wonderful plan my boy! Gentlemen, please follow this young man out. He'll show you to your lodgings and will hear all your complaints and entreaties."

Nikki watched nervously as the men from the Mystic Mountains followed Rufius out of the council chamber. The King's guards brought up the rear, their spears at the ready. Watching the guards, so ready to defend the King, Nikki wondered how Rufius had gotten the Mystic men into the castle in the first place. She doubted the guards at the front gate would have let them in without his help. And not just into the castle, but all the way into the King's council chamber. The Mystic men didn't exactly look like peaceful citizens who'd come to discuss the taxes on their farms.

"Well," said the King to his advisors. "that was odd. Far be it from me to criticize any citizen of the Realm, but those chaps seemed a trifle rough and uncultured. Also a few of them were definitely in need of a bath. One of them had flies circling his head. Normally my more junior advisors catch this type of thing before it comes to my attention. I'd never have a minute's peace if I had to be available for every minor complaint. Still, I'm sure Rufius will handle the matter with his usual competence. Poor old Mally certainly knew what he was doing when he made that young man his assistant. I think that concludes our discussions for today. Thank you gentlemen."

The King's advisors filed out, leaving Nikki and Curio alone in the room with the King.

Nikki pulled her page's hat off, determined to talk to the King before she lost her nerve. She stepped away from the wall and cleared her throat. "Hello, your Highness," she said. "Perhaps you don't remember me. My name's Nikki. We met for the first time here at Castle Cogent, in your rose garden. Right after Athena and Fuzz brought me to the Realm."

The King looked at her in surprise. "Why yes, young lady. Of course I remember you. We don't often get visitors coming through the portal anymore. I didn't realize you were still in the Realm. I hope you have been enjoying your visit here."

"Well, no, I haven't," said Nikki. "I don't mean to be rude, but things have been going very badly in the Realm, as I'm sure your Highness realizes."

The King looked more surprised at this remark than he did at the sudden entrance of the men from the Mystic Mountains. "Very badly? What on earth do you mean, young lady? Granted, our levels of education have slipped since my father's reign. I believe that was why my emissaries Athena and Fuzz brought you here in the first place. But other than that little trifle I have noticed no difficulties here in the Realm. Not unless you mean the usual squabbles between the turnip farmers and the pig farmers. Every year the turnip farmers come to the castle to complain that all their turnips are being eaten, and every year I tell them that pigs like turnips. It is as simple as that. If you know of any other problems in the Realm you should report them to Rufius. He is a wizard at solving problems. The Realm has been expertly managed ever since he took over the position Maleficious held. Now, if you'll excuse me, I have an appointment with my healer. I have a bit of a sore shoulder from playing lawn tennis yesterday."

The King left, leaving Nikki and Curio staring after him with open mouths.

"This is not good, Miss," said Curio. "The King seems to have handed the ruling of the Realm over to Poofius."

"Yes," said Nikki, flopping down into one of the leather-backed chairs around the council table. She sat there twisting her page's hat in her hands, while Curio nervously paced back and forth across the room.

"Any ideas yet, Miss?" asked Curio after ten minutes of pacing.

"No," said Nikki. She stared at the floor and tried to clear her mind. Her math teacher back at Westlake High School had taught her to use four steps when faced with a difficult problem. First, make sure you understand the problem. Second, collect data. Third, analyze the data to make sure it's accurate and relevant to the problem. Fourth, determine your plan of action. After months spent in the Realm she was pretty sure she had enough data. The first step was trickier. What problem exactly was she trying to solve? In math class problems were laid out nice and neat on the blackboard or on a test. In real life problems were a lot messier. She decided that there were two big problems in the Realm. The first was the increasing prejudice faced by the imps and the invasion of their homeland of ImpHaven. The second was Rufius trying to grab power and set himself up as the ruler of the Realm. The first problem seemed to be caused by the second. She wasn't naïve enough to think that Rufius was the only person in the Realm who was a bigot when it came to the imps, but he was definitely making use of that bigotry to gain power. So, Rufius was the problem she needed to focus on. It was a shame that the Realm was a monarchy and not a democracy. In a democracy there would be other sources of power. She could go to the parliament or the senate to find allies against Rufius. And allies were desperately needed. Rufius now controlled both the Knights of the Iron Fist and the men from the Mystic Mountains. Okay, so she had the first step completed. She'd identified Rufius as the problem. Now for the fourth step, the plan of action. The nobles of the Realm were a possibility she hadn't considered before. After the King they had the most power and the most wealth. Some of the nobles were probably shallow people like Gwen's mother, Lady Ursula, with her pink poodle and her obsession with fancy clothes. But some of them were probably decent people like the Prince of Physics. The problem was that Lady Ursula and the Prince were the only two nobles she'd met in the Realm. She wished Gwen was at Castle Cogent. Gwen had given up her status as a noble, but she could still contact her mother, who probably knew every nobleman and noblewoman in the entire Realm.

Nikki looked up as Cation suddenly appeared in the open doorway, a dead mouse in her teeth. She dropped the mouse at Nikki's feet and jumped into her lap.

Nikki sighed and scratched the kitten under her chin. "I wish Cation could lead us to Athena and Fuzz. They must be here somewhere. I'm sure they have some kind of plan for how to deal with Rufius."

"Our best bet for finding them, if they're here, is the lower levels, Miss," said Curio, still pacing. "It'd be very difficult for Miss Athena and Mr. Fuzz to remain hidden up here in the formal rooms of the castle. Lots of guards and courtiers wandering about all day. And being imps they'd stick out. I believe imps used to work here in the castle not long ago, but I'd bet my big toe that Poofius has fired them all."

"Okay," said Nikki, putting her page's hat back on and tucking her hair under it. "Let's go back down to the Page House. But let's skip those blasted never-ending stairs and take the other route Mick mentioned. The outside route through the courtyards and tunnels. I want to have a look at the rest of the castle. I especially want to check out what the castle guards are doing. They seem like they're still loyal to the King, but if Rufius gets control of them we're in real trouble."

They cautiously wandered through the tapestry-covered halls and marble-floored passageways of the upper level of Castle Cogent, trying to find a way out to the rose garden and its tunnel down to the lower levels. Castle Cogent had beautiful white-marble walls inside as well as out, with vases of roses, tulips and peonies overflowing from every corner. Despite the guards everywhere it was much more a pleasure palace than the Southern Castle in Kingston. The castle in Kingston was more of a military fortress, with its rough stone walls and endless dungeons.

They passed groups of gossiping courtiers hanging around in the passageways wearing fine silks and jewels. The courtiers took no notice of them. Patrolling guards with spears on their shoulders marched past but didn't give them a second glance. Nikki and Curio were just two anonymous pages with a stray cat following at their heels.

As they passed a group of courtiers who were gossiping next to a white marble vase full of lilacs Nikki paused and stared at them. For some reason it had never occurred to her that the courtiers who hung around Castle Cogent all day must be members of the nobility.

A man in a sky-blue silk jacket and pantaloons noticed her staring. "Yes?" he barked impatiently. "Is there a message for me?"

"What?" said Nikki. "Um, no. Sorry sir. Just admiring the lilacs."

Nikki and Curio hurried past.

"What was that about, Miss?" whispered Curio. "Not a terribly interesting bunch to catch your eye, if you ask me. Same as all the other hangers-on who spend all day trying to get close to the King."

"He looked like a noble," said Nikki. "Are all the courtiers here at the castle members of the nobility?"

"I think so, Miss," said Curio. "Once in a while you'll get a rich merchant like Avaricious hanging around these halls, but merchants are busy. They've got their businesses to look after, so mostly they stay in D-ville, where all the money-lending and trading goes on. The nobles, now, they got nothing to do all day. So they hangs around the castle hoping to catch the eye of the King to ask him favors."

Nikki nodded, wondering how on earth she could approach one of the courtiers. She could pretend to have a message for one of them, but she had no way of knowing which of them were connected with Rufius. She was certain some of them were. He'd probably passed out bribes right and left in the castle. No, trying to talk to the courtiers at random was too dangerous. She had to have a way in. Someone who knew them. Carmela was a possibility. Since she managed the King's household she undoubtedly knew everyone at Castle Cogent.

"This way, Miss," said Curio. "I can see rose bushes out of this window. I think these stairs go outside."

They hurried down a short spiral staircase and emerged into the sunlight.

Nikki paused to let her eyes adjust to the brightness. They were on the edge of the rose garden in the main courtyard of the castle. In the distance she could see jets of water splashing into the sky from the marble fountain shaped like a salmon. The same fountain where Athena and Fuzz had introduced her to the King so many months ago. On a patch of smooth lawn nearby there were targets set up for what looked like archery practice. A cluster of guards stood on the lawn making adjustments to some kind of equipment. Courtiers sat on white marble benches surrounding the lawn, sipping out of silver goblets and watching the guards.

Cation, who had been patiently following at their heels, darted forward into the sunshine and chased after a monarch butterfly fluttering among the rose bushes.

Nikki and Curio inched forward to get a closer look at what the guards were doing. By standing on tip toe to peer over the top of a yellow rose bush Nikki could see that the guards were fiddling with some kind of crossbow. It was extremely lethal-looking and the guards were having a hard time loading a bolt into it. It took two of them just to pull back the cable which controlled the launching of the bolt. There was a hand-crank attached to the stock which pulled back the cable, but it seemed to be broken. A guard tried to turn the crank, but a spring fell out onto the lawn and screws and bits of wood flew everywhere.

"You! Go get old Geber!" yelled one of the guards, pointing at Nikki. "His blasted contraption is busted again!"

Nikki looked behind her, hoping that the guard was addressing someone else.

"Yeah, I mean you, page!" yelled the guard. "And be quick about it!"

Nikki gave an awkward salute and scurried away, Curio following.

"He must mean the old alchemist," said Nikki. "I met Geber in Deceptionville when I got separated from you and Fuzz and Athena. I wonder what he's doing in Castle Cogent?"

"Don't know, Miss," said Curio, dodging a gardener who was pulling weeds out of the lawn. "But we better go find him quick. We don't want no trouble with the guards. Right now nobody's paying us any attention cause of these page uniforms, but that can change right quick if we rub somebody the wrong way."

"We can't search the whole castle for Geber," said Nikki. "Where do you think he might be?"

"My guess would be the workshops, Miss. I knows Geber from my D-ville days. Not personally, of course. But everyone in D-ville knows old Geber and his potions and contraptions. Chief Alchemist, he used to call himself. Let's try those workshops we came past when Mick brought us up to Carmela's quarters."

They headed back into the labyrinth of passageways in the castle. At the top of the spiral stairs Cation mewed pitifully, scratching at Nikki's leg until Nikki scooped her up and placed the kitten on her shoulder. Cation immediately dug her claws into the velvet page's uniform, got a nice firm grip and began purring loudly in Nikki's ear.

After going up and down uncountable marble staircases, along luxurious corridors lined with mirrors and vases of roses, and past hordes of gossiping courtiers they finally worked their way down to the storage rooms and workshops. All manner of workers were cutting leather and carving wood and sewing clothes and polishing silver and blowing glass to make goblets and vases, but they saw no sign of an alchemists' workshop. Finally Curio snagged a passing page.

"Hey," said Curio, "Do you knows where we might find an old man called Geber? He messes around with potions and stuff. We has a message for him."

"Do I know you?" asked the page, looking down his nose at Curio as he fluffed the two feathers in his page cap. "I thought I knew every page in the castle. Also you look too much of a half-pint to be a page. Are they hiring from the nursery now?"

"We're in training," said Nikki in a gruff voice. "Do you know where Geber is or not?"

"Yeah, I know," said the page over his shoulder as he walked away. "He's a big cheese, he is. Got his own quarters up in the top level, near the throne room. Good luck trying to get in there."

Curio stuck his tongue out at the page's back. "Stupid two-feather. Them with two-feathers in their caps are a little bit senior to the one-feathers, so they think they're practically as important as the King hisself. They treated me like dirt last time I was here with me master. Should'a kicked him in the shins."

"No you shouldn't have," said Nikki as they headed back up to the upper levels. "We're trying to keep a low profile, remember. The last thing we want is a page mad at us. He'd bad-mouth us all over the page house and get us kicked out and we don't want that. These page costumes have been working out great. We can go anywhere in the castle."

"Yer right, Miss," said Curio a bit grumpily. "I won't punch Mr. Two-Feathers in the nose next time I see him, no matter how high that big nose is in the air." He pointed down a passageway whose floor was covered with black and white tiles. "This way, Miss. I remember this led to that council chamber we was in. The throne room should be near that."

They heard Geber before they saw him. A door burst open at the end of the hallway and a ceramic pot came flying out of the door. It smashed against the far wall, shards flying everywhere. Nikki winced as a sharp piece hit her on the cheek, drawing blood. Cation yowled and jumped down from Nikki's shoulder. She dashed behind a large malachite vase filled with marigolds and hid there, growling.

"I wouldn't go in there if I was you," said a young man, hurrying out the door. "He's in a throwing mood. Got me good." He pointed to the smelly brown liquid dripping from his hair and down onto his tattered shirt and pants. "Got to go down to the baths and clean me self up before this stuff hardens and I has to shave me head. Wouldn't be the first time. Last year he threw some wet plaster at me. It set rock-hard before I could dunk me head in the D-ville river."

Nikki gasped and pulled her page hat low over her face. It was Sandor, Geber's assistant. She'd last seen him in Deceptionville, when he'd helped her escape from a Lurker who'd cornered her in the Wolf's Hide tavern. Despite his help that day she'd never been entirely sure whether he was friend or foe. He seemed to veer wildly from crude and abusive to helpful and sympathetic. She wondered if he had some kind of personality disorder. This time, whatever his problem was, she needn't have worried about being recognized. Sandor stomped off without so much as a second glance at her.

Nikki and Curio cautiously peeked around the door he'd come out of. The luxurious quarters looked like Carmela's, with heavy oak furniture and red velvet drapes at the tall windows. Competing with the sunlight streaming in were candelabras as tall as a man. Each was tucked into a corner of the room and burned fat, smoky candles. Workbenches had been installed along the paneled walls. Steam was rising from bubbling glass flasks and a strong smell of sulfur stained the air.

"Well, what is it?" snapped an old man sitting on a stool in front of the nearest workbench. He was untangling a quill from his long white beard. "If you've brought a message from that little brat Rufius you can just go back and tell him it will be ready when I say it's ready and not a moment before."

Nikki nudged Curio, giving him a little push towards Geber. She knew from her time in Deceptionville City Hall that Geber's eyesight wasn't good, still, he might recognize her if she got too close.

"No sir," said Curio with an awkward little bow. "We've been sent by the castle guards. They been having some trouble with one of their weapons. Seems it's broken and you are the only one who can fix it."

Geber sighed deeply. He climbed slowly off the stool and fumbled for his cane, which was hanging from the workbench. "And I suppose that you didn't have the foresight to bring the offending item with you?"

"Um, no sir," said Curio. "I don't think the guards want us pages wandering around the castle with weapons. We might revolt cause of the lousy food they serves us down in the page house. We had what they called lamb stew last night, but between you and me I think more'n a few cats made it into the pot."

Geber gave a wheezy laugh. "I wouldn't be at all surprised, my boy. Not at all. The office boys in D-ville City Hall are often fed pigeon pie, and it's not plump, farm-raised doves that they're eating. It's the flea-infested birds that poop on the statue of the mayor down in the main square." He crooked an arthritic finger at Curio. "Come here, boy. I'll give you a quick glance at my latest project as a reward for being such an amusing messenger."

Curio stepped forward hesitantly. The flask Geber had been sitting in front of was giving off billowing puffs of foul-smelling steam.

Geber picked up a pair of iron tongs and lifted the flask off the flame burning beneath it. His hand shook so much that a drop of liquid inside the flask splashed onto the workbench. Within seconds the drop had burned straight through the heavy wooden bench and dropped onto the stone floor where it sizzled angrily. Geber set the flask down on a stone tile nearby and snatched up a small pot filled with powder. He dumped the powder on the floor and the sizzling stopped.

"Notice the smell, boy?" asked Geber. "Can you tell me what it is?"

Curio sniffed. "Pine, I think. Smells like the pine tar that the carpenters in D-ville use to waterproof the roofs of the noble's houses."

Geber nodded. "But not just pine tar. I've added a few things to it. Things to make it burn faster and hotter. The King's guards can dip an arrow in this, light it, and burn down a three-story house in minutes."

"And why would they want to do that, sir?" asked Curio. "I don't think the King's subjects would want their houses burned down. Seems like it would be inconvenient."

Geber shrugged. "I'm just the King's Chief Alchemist. My task is to invent the weapons the King wants. What he does with them is his business."

"The King told you he wanted this?" asked Nikki in the gruffest voice she could manage.

"Yes, of course," said Geber impatiently, giving her an angry, near-sighted glance. "Rufius brought me the King's request only yesterday. I verified it with the Captain of the Castle Guard, of course. I never trust anything that little brat Rufian tells me. His heart is as black as that ridiculous tunic he wears. Captain Voltan assured me that the request came straight from the King."

Nikki eyed the smoking spot on the floor warily. She could smell more than just pine. There was a distinct smell of garlic coming from the spot. And the smoke was unusually thick and white. Her skin began to crawl as a thought crept into her mind. White Phosphorous. It was an allotrope of the element phosphorous and was extremely flammable. It had a strong garlicky smell and it emitted dense smoke when heated. It was created by heating the calcium phosphate present in phosphate rock. Her History teacher had told their class about it when they'd studied World War I. It had mainly been used for smoke screens, so that troops could sneak up on an enemy, but it had also been used in chemical warfare and could kill when it was breathed in. It was so dangerous that it had been banned by international chemical weapons treaties. She reached out and snagged the back of Curio's page jacket, pulling him away from the smoke.

Geber noticed, and with a small smile plopped a pewter mug over the spot, containing the smoke. "Not to worry," he said. "That little bit of smoke won't hurt you. Now, lead me to these guards and their broken toy."

Their trip back to the rose garden took much longer this time, with Geber pausing to rest on his cane every twenty feet. When they reached the spiral stairs which led out to the garden he refused to go down them. Nikki and Curio had to fetch two guards to carry the old alchemist down, sitting in their linked arms like a child in a swing.

When they reached the rose garden a tall guard with a purple feather waving from his helmet strode up to them.

"Here you are at last Geber," he barked. "What took you so long? My men have been standing by, idle as a pack of pigs drunk on Cogent Town ale."

"And why is this my problem?" asked Geber, motioning irritably for the guards to put him down. "The idleness of your men is not my concern, Captain Voltan. I am the King's Chief Alchemist, not your lackey. Your guards should learn to fix their own weapons. Surely there is someone among them with a little mechanical aptitude."

Captain Voltan snorted. "My men have enough trouble putting their shoes on the right feet. The quality of the recruits has dropped considerably since a certain Rufian took over the running of Castle Cogent."

"Well, you will just have to manage," said Geber hobbling up to the men who were milling aimlessly on the grass in the middle of the rose garden. "Hand it here, my boy," he snapped at the guard holding the broken crossbow.

The guard handed it to him and Geber teetered over to a nearby bench with it. He imperiously waved a courtier off the bench and plopped down, nearly impaling himself with the crossbow's razor-sharp, steel-shafted bolt. Muttering to himself, he removed the bolt and peered near-sightedly at the weapon.

Nikki casually positioned herself behind him and peeked over his shoulder. There was a kind of winch attached to the stock of the crossbow which looked like it was used to tighten the firing string. The winch had a handle similar to a child's Jack-in-the-Box. Instead of a bowman pulling the string back by hand he would wind the winch. The wound-up winch stored potential energy, and when the trigger was pulled the potential energy was converted to kinetic energy which propelled the bolt. A winch could generate more force than pulling with your fingers, but it looked like this one was broken. It hung off the stock at a crazy angle. A toothed metal rod about a foot long ran along the stock and entered the winch. Nikki saw right away what was the matter. There was a ring of metal pegs inside the winch which caught the teeth of the metal rod. This was how the string was pulled tight. The mechanism was similar to an old-fashioned watch with gears, or to a music box which was wound by hand. In each case there was a kind of gear-and-peg arrangement. In this case several of the pegs inside the winch had broken off and the string could no longer be tightened.

Geber put his nose down until it was almost touching the winch, but it was clear he was having trouble seeing well enough to diagnose the problem.

Nikki certainly wasn't going to tell him. In addition to not wanting to call attention to herself she was happy that the weapon was broken. The metal, arrow-like bolts looked horribly lethal. She guessed that when the crossbow was in working order that it could shoot a bolt right through the wall of a house. She didn't know how common this type of weapon was in the Realm, but she wasn't going to help fix this one.

"Well?" snapped Captain Voltan. "Can you fix it or not? Little Rufian wants the castle workshops to start making dozens of these weapons, but that is pointless if they don't even work."

"Of course I can fix it, fool," said Geber, not bothering to look up. "I've been the Chief Alchemist of the Realm longer than you've been alive. I can fix anything. I just need a clearer view of the problem. Have one of your men run to my chambers and fetch me my box of lenses. It's a small wooden box covered in blue leather."

Captain Voltan gestured to a nearby guard. The guard ran off toward the spiral staircase leading to the upper levels of the castle.

Nikki and Curio backed cautiously away from Geber and took up a position behind a yellow rose bush while they decided what to do. Nikki was smelling one of the roses when loud barking erupted behind her. She turned to see a little black dog chasing a mouse around the garden.

"Toby!" she gasped.

Curio turned to look. "Miss Gwen's dog from D-ville? Are you sure, Miss?" he asked. "There's lots of black dogs in the Realm."

"I'm sure," said Nikki. "See? He has the collar Gwen made for him. It has that little silver heart hanging off it."

"Gosh, you're right, Miss," said Curio. "Do ya think it means Miss Gwen is here in the castle?"

"She must be," said Nikki, scanning the garden as if Gwen was about to suddenly pop up out of the ground. "She must have come here from ImpHaven with Athena and Fuzz."

"Miss," said Curio, "I think we're getting a bit ahead of ourselves. All we got is a cat and a dog. Maybe Cation and Toby got here on their own somehows. I heard tell of a cat that got itself stuck in a basket of apples and travelled all the way from D-ville to Kingston on the back of a horse-cart. It was a sorry, scrawny little beast by the time it arrived, but it travelled hundreds of miles without its owner anywheres around."

Nikki waved an impatient hand at him. "No. Gwen's here. And Athena and Fuzz are too. I just know it." She glanced thoughtfully up at the tall white battlements surrounding the rose garden. The castle's purple and gold flags were flapping in the breeze, either gracefully or arrogantly depending on your point of view. "My guess is that it's too dangerous for them to stay in the castle. The King would welcome Athena and Fuzz, but Rufius would have them thrown in the dungeons as soon as the King's back was turned. I bet they're hiding somewhere down in Cogent Town."

"Maybe," said Curio doubtfully. "But how are we gonna find them?"

Nikki watched Toby as the small dog chased the mouse under a rose bush and started digging frantically. "We'll follow Toby."

Chapter Seven

Cats and Dogs

"**D**ARN IT!" GASPED Nikki. She slid to a halt and snatched up her Nikes, which had fallen out of her page uniform. She stuffed the shoes back under her purple velvet tunic and resumed running. Toby was setting a blistering pace. It was as if the small dog had heard some kind of urgent call from Gwen and was rushing to her side. It was dinner time and the steep road down from the castle was empty. Nikki and Curio puffed along, trying to keep Toby in sight. They'd had no trouble getting out of the castle. The guards at the drawbridge had barely glanced up as they ran by.

By the time the castle road joined with the main street of Cogent Town both Nikki and Curio were clutching their sides and gasping for breath. Nikki winced as her borrowed leather shoes slapped on the cobblestones. She was used to more padding on her feet when she ran and sparks of pain were shooting up her legs. Fortunately Toby chose that moment to slow to a walk. He stopped next to the watering-trough in front of a tavern and turned to look back at them. He gave a short bark.

"Do ya think he recognizes us, Miss?" asked Curio. "Seems like he doesn't mind us following him."

"I guess it's possible," said Nikki. "We did spend a lot of time with him and Gwen in her rooms in Deceptionville, when she was still working at that shop belonging to Avaricious."

Toby sniffed at a bedraggled lilac bush outside the tavern. It looked like it had been watered by all the dogs in Cogent Town. After satisfying his nose he set off again. They followed closely on his heels as he led them through Cogent Town's darkening side streets and back alleys. He seemed to consider himself on some kind of mission, even refusing to bark at a calico cat which hissed at him from the window of a butcher shop.

They lost sight of Toby for a moment when he suddenly darted through a mass of vines hanging from a stone archway. When they pushed through the vines they saw him scratching at a door which was half off its hinges. The door creaked open and a blonde head appeared, tinged with blue in the moonlight.

"Gwen!" whispered Nikki.

Gwen's head jerked up and her eyes narrowed as she peered through the gloom.

"Hello Miss Gwen," said Curio, stepping out of the shadows. "Do ya think you could let us in? Probably best if we don't hang around outside yer hideout. We might attract the wrong sort of attention."

Gwen gave a quick look around the vine-covered alley then waved them inside, giving each of them a hug. She shooed Toby through the door before dragging it shut again. "This way," she whispered, leading them up a narrow wooden staircase. "Watch your step. Some of the boards are rotted. Our hideout as you call it is not exactly a palace. It's a wonder the roof hasn't caved in on our heads."

At the top of the stairs Gwen stopped on a tiny landing and pulled an iron key from her pocket. The key was nearly as big as her hand. "Our security," she said with a grin. "If the locked door doesn't stop them we'll just hit them on the head with this key." She waved them inside and locked the door behind them. "Make yourselves at home. Fuzz is out 'borrowing' something for our dinner and Athena is taking a nap. I'll go wake her."

Nikki looked around the small room. A single candle was burning in a glass jar perched on an upturned bucket. There was no furniture, just an array of buckets, pans, and washtubs on the floor, all full of water. Nikki looked up. Water from last night's rain was still dripping from the ceiling.

"Miss, it is so good to see you again." Athena came into the room. She had a tattered shawl wrapped around her grey woolen dress. One of her legs dragged as she walked.

"Athena!" gasped Nikki, "what happened?"

The imp reached up and patted Nikki's hand. "Do not worry, Miss. It is only a minor injury."

Gwen's blue eyes flashed angrily. "She was hit by an arrow as we were retreating from ImpHaven. Fortunately Linnea was able to treat the wound so that it didn't become infected. She flushed it with witch hazel steeped in alcohol, then cauterized it."

Nikki winced. Cauterizing meant burning the wound with boiling oil or red-hot metal. It was an old and painful way of preventing infection before the discovery of antibiotics.

Curio jumped as a drop of water landed on his head.

Gwen brushed the drop off his hair. "Come on everyone. Let's go into the bedroom and get comfortable. We've got lots to discuss."

They crowded into the bedroom, which was even tinier than the front room. Three beds were crammed in side-by-side and took up all the floor space. Nikki and Gwen helped Athena into the bed by the window and then sat cross-legged on the two other beds. Curio perched on the rickety frame at the end of Athena's bed, tucking his feet under the patchwork quilt.

"So," said Gwen, folding her hands in her lap. "You're probably wondering what happened in ImpHaven after you left."

Nikki nodded warily, not sure she wanted to know.

Gwen noticed Nikki's tense expression. She nodded. "Yes, there were deaths," she said bluntly.

Nikki and Curio both drew in sharp breaths.

"Tarn was killed," said Gwen. "He was impaled by a spear while defending Athena's mother's house. He was one of the last to retreat. His bravery allowed most of the imps sheltering in the house to escape out the back, including Athena's mother and Aunt Gertie. Linnea also escaped."

Nikki sighed in relief at the news that Linnea was okay, though she felt an uncomfortable twinge of guilt about Tarn. She'd never liked the imp, not since the day she'd met him on the south coast of the Realm along with the rest of Griff's crew. She'd always had the impression that he didn't like non-imps. It was hard not to take that personally. But considering how the imps were being treated in the Realm she couldn't really blame him. And despite her dislike she'd certainly never wished him dead.

"Triton was also killed," said Gwen. "ImpHaven's Harbormaster and head of their Watch. He led the Watch in a charge against a pack of knights who were burning down houses in the capital, near the harbor. It was sticks and fishing nets against armed knights on horseback. The imps managed to drag a few knights off their horses, but in the end there was no hope. Many of the Watch were killed. I'm afraid I don't know their names."

"Floyd the butcher's son, Damon from the coast, Tillon who was a friend of my mother's and too old to be fighting," said Athena wearily. She was leaning against the wall with her eyes closed. "Linnea would know all the names. She tended to the wounded and the dying."

Gwen nodded sadly. "After so many of the Watch were killed Fuzz and Athena took temporary control of ImpHaven City and ordered everyone to evacuate. Most of the imps left the city and hid in ImpHaven's forests, but some have left the Realm entirely. A large group paid for passage on a merchant ship which was anchored off of ImpHaven harbor and sailed for the Southern Isles. Linnea tried to convince them not to. She's had many dealings with traders from the

Southern Isles and she knows of the tropical diseases there. Newcomers to the Isles can become very sick and even die just from drinking the water, but the imps could not be dissuaded. They sailed and more are planning to follow them. It is horribly sad, but I don't blame them for leaving the Realm. I would leave too if I were treated so badly."

Nikki didn't know how to respond to such sad news, but she was spared having to reply by the sound of a key turning in the front door. Toby dashed out of the bedroom, barking furiously.

"Quiet down, you mangy mutt. The neighbors will complain and set the Rounders on us."

Fuzz entered the bedroom and dumped a lumpy burlap sack on the nearest bed. If he was surprised at the sight of Nikki and Curio he didn't show it. "Got us a nice roasted chicken and some boiled potatoes. They're cold but that's not gonna stop me. I'm so hungry I could eat old Toby here."

Toby growled fiercely, but his eyes never left the burlap sack.

"Yeah, yeah," said Fuzz opening the sack. "I got you some mutton, you worthless furball. After your dinner why don't you earn your keep by catching a few rats. I found one curled up on my chest when I woke up this morning." He threw the scraps of mutton into the front room and Toby dashed after them.

"So," said Fuzz as he climbed onto the nearest bed, pulled out a pocketknife and began cutting up the chicken, "now that we're all back together again have we decided on a plan?"

Gwen shook her head. "We haven't got that far yet. I've just been catching Nikki and Curio up on the ImpHaven situation."

Fuzz's expression hardened and he flicked a worried glance in Athena's direction. "Maybe we should move on from that gloomy topic and focus on Krill."

"Krill?" said Nikki in surprise. "Is he here?"

Fuzz nodded and passed her a drumstick. "Rufius had him brought here from ImpHaven. He's in the castle dungeon."

"Kira's here too," said Gwen. "We caught sight of her briefly, buying bread at a market stall here in Cogent Town. But she disappeared into the crowd before we could catch up to her. We've been trying to find her. We're sure she's going to try and rescue her brother, but it would be better if she joined forces with us rather than going it alone."

"Is the rest of Griff's crew here?" asked Nikki.

"No," said Fuzz. "I've got friends here in Cogent Town, and they haven't heard anything about a bunch of pirates wandering the streets. Griff and her crew tend to stick out. They smell like codfish for one thing. If they were here we'd know about it."

"That's too bad," said Nikki. "We need as many allies as we can get. What about the Prince of Physics. Have you heard from him? Kira was going to try and contact him."

Fuzz shook his head. "Things have been a mess since the invasion of ImpHaven. Our usual sources of information have dried up. People are scared to talk now that Rufius is in power. And they're especially scared to talk to an imp. I've heard a few rumors that the Prince is still trapped on his estate in Kingston, surrounded by the Knights of the Iron Fist. I don't think we can count on any help from him just now."

"What about Darius?" asked Nikki. "Did they throw him in the dungeon with Krill?"

Gwen's pale face turned beet red and she looked down at her lap.

"Darius is up at the castle," said Fuzz, his face rigid with anger, "but he's not in the dungeons. Rufius gave him a post as Chief Stonemason of Castle Cogent. He's got rooms in the Stonemasons' Guild down on the lower level of the castle."

"I don't understand," said Nikki. "Is he pretending to cooperate with Rufius? So he can spy on him or something?"

Fuzz shot a quick look at Gwen, who was still staring down at her lap. "I don't think so. There are still a few imps left in Cogent Town. Imps who run important businesses that would be hard to replace if they were shut down. Lens makers, wood carvers, tool makers, glass blowers. I talked to a glass blower who used to live in the town Darius comes from. He said that Darius is known to be a separatist. Separatists are people who believe that imps and non-imps should live apart from each other. Separatists don't hate the imps, but they do believe it's okay to drive the imps out of the Realm. They think we should all leave the Realm and go live in ImpHaven. But Rufius's invasion of ImpHaven has mucked up that neat little plan."

Nikki stared at Fuzz, her mouth hanging open. "I had no idea," she finally stammered. "Darius always seemed like such a nice person. He helped us rescue Aunt Gertie and lots of other imps from the dungeons of the Southern Castle. And he helped defend ImpHaven during the invasion."

"He *is* a nice person," snapped Gwen, her blue eyes flashing angrily. "He just has some odd ideas."

Fuzz snorted. "I'd call the separatists nasty rather than odd. Granted, they're not as out-and-out evil as someone like Rufius, but their obsession with dividing people into groups and forcing them to live apart has caused a lot of suffering for the imps. We've always had trouble from non-imps, even those who aren't separatists. Our size and our small population makes us a convenient target. That's why it's so important for us to have someone like the Prince of Physics or the King on our side. Someone who has the power to stand up for us when it counts. Speaking of the King, Gwen told us you two came here to try and talk to the King. How's that going?"

"We did manage a brief conversation with the King," said Nikki. "A friend of Curio's got us these page uniforms. Once we put these on we found out we could go anywhere in the castle. People just ignored us as if we were invisible. Anyway, we got assigned messenger duty, which got us inside the King's council chamber while he was having a meeting with his advisers." She hesitated.

"And?" said Fuzz impatiently.

"I kind of accosted him after the meeting, when everyone else had left. The King seems to think that Rufius is doing a wonderful job of governing the Realm," Nikki said reluctantly. "I tried, but I don't think I made much of an impression on him. He said the Realm was doing fine except for some spats between pig farmers and turnip farmers, and then he left because his shoulder hurt from playing lawn tennis."

"Poor thing," said Athena weakly, her eyes still closed. "I hope his Majesty will soon recover."

Fuzz looked like he was about to explode with rage, but one look at Athena's white face and he swallowed whatever he was about to say.

Nikki also tamped down an angry response. She was beginning to realize that Athena viewed the King as a kind of son. A favored, spoiled son who could do no wrong. It was kind of sweet, but it also created a huge problem for them. The King was one of the few people in the Realm capable of standing up to Rufius and removing him from power, but she now realized that he just wasn't up to the task. And Athena, who was probably closer to him than anyone in the Realm, wouldn't insist that he try. She'd make excuses for him and brush away any accusations that he was a weak and lazy ruler. She glanced at Fuzz, but he just shrugged as if to say he'd been over this topic with Athena and it had done no good.

Nikki sighed. "Well, apart from the tragedy of the King's tennis injury, something else happened at the council meeting. The Mystic Men marched in. That's just what I call them. I don't know what they're actually called. They're this weird group of men who live in a really remote fortress way up in the Mystic Mountains. I got kind of captured by them when I was trying to find my way back to Kingston."

"Oh, Miss!" gasped Athena, her eyes flying open. "What happened? Were you hurt?"

"No, no," said Nikki, waving her hands reassuringly. "They didn't hurt me. I just kind of stumbled across their territory by mistake. Actually, I got swept over a waterfall and landed in their valley. They found me and took me to their headman. He was a creepy guy, that's for sure. Bald guy, with a missing eye. Just an empty eye socket with a vein in it which pulsed when he was angry, which seemed to be all the time. There was a large portrait of Maleficious painted on the wall of their fortress. They seemed to kind of worship him. Apparently he gave them some land or something. Anyway, I told them that Maleficious was dead, and that a lot of people thought Rufius had killed him. I was trying to rile them up so they would go away and leave me alone, which is exactly what they did. They yelled and stamped and shook their knives and rushed out of the fortress shouting for revenge against Rufius. So I was super surprised today when they suddenly marched into the King's council chamber with Rufius. Their headman and Rufius now seem like best pals, which is extremely weird since back in the Mystic Mountains the headman was screaming that he wanted Rufius's head on a platter."

Fuzz just blinked at her. He looked like he was having trouble processing this new information. Finally he cleared his throat. "Huh. I'm trying to decide if this helps us or hurts us. I've never heard of these Mystic Men before." He looked at Athena, but she shook her head.

"No, nor have I," she said. "I have been a King's Emissary all my life, but I have never been assigned to travel in the Mystic Mountains. Not many citizens of the Realm go there. It is a harsh land with very tall jagged peaks and deep narrow valleys that people sometimes get trapped in. It sounds like these men are outlaws, so the Mystics would be a good place for them to hide in. They could live for years without being found, and it seems they have done just that."

"And now they've apparently joined forces with Rufius," said Fuzz, rubbing his unshaven jaw thoughtfully. "How many of these

Mystic Men are there?"

Nikki shrugged. "I don't know. There were about a hundred in their fortress in the mountains, but I got the impression that there were more of them living in the valley below. But just men, I think. No women or children. They seem to be a kind of gang, not an actual community."

Fuzz nodded. "That's good. Sounds like they're limited in numbers. We've got enough problems without thousands of newcomers joining up with Rufius."

Toby ran into the bedroom just then and jumped up on Gwen's bed. The little dog licked her hand and settled down with his head in her lap. Gwen smiled faintly and scratched his back.

"How did Toby get here?" asked Nikki. "I thought you left him at your mother's house when you quit your job in Deceptionville."

"I did," said Gwen. "Mother brought him here. She's in Cogent Town visiting an old friend of hers, the Duchess of Falsa. Mother pays her a visit every year around this time."

"Huh," said Nikki, thinking quickly. Gwen's mother, Lady Ursula, Duchess of Malaprop, was the ideal person to use as a contact to the nobility of the Realm. And Gwen herself was technically a member of the nobility, though she'd given up that life. "Have you seen her?" Nikki asked. "Your mother, I mean. I know you didn't part on great terms, but she probably misses you."

Gwen shrugged. "Maybe. It's hard to tell with mother sometimes. She isn't very affectionate. When I still lived at home in Muddled Manor she spent most of her time criticizing my appearance. Appearances are very important to mother. A daughter who was never interested in ball gowns and who spent all her time in the basement mixing chemicals was a huge disappointment. Also, she was horrified when I got a job in D-ville. The daughter of a noblewoman isn't supposed to work for a living."

"Still, I think you should go visit her," said Nikki.

"Why?" asked Gwen.

It was Nikki's turn to blush. "Because it could be very helpful to us. To the imps. Look, I know it sounds like I want to use you and your mom. Well, to be honest, I kind of do. But it's for a good cause. The imps need allies. And their two biggest allies, the King and the Prince of Physics, are kind of out of commission right now. The King is not standing up to Rufius and the Prince is trapped down in Kingston. Nobles like your mom have a lot of power in the Realm. They could put a lot of pressure on the King if they wanted to. Some of them are probably anti-imp, but I bet some of them aren't. I bet some of them are good people. Even the courtiers who hang around all day up at the castle can't be all bad."

Gwen was silent for a minute. "Bertie is staying with the Duchess of Falsa," she finally said.

"Oh!" exclaimed Athena, a bit of color coming back into her white face. "Bertie! Of course. Why didn't I think of that!"

"Who's Bertie?" asked Nikki.

"He is the King's nephew," said Athena. "He has been travelling outside of the Realm for the last several years. He is a dear little boy."

Fuzz snorted. "He's a dear little ass. An empty-headed fool if there ever was one. And he's not so little. Not anymore. He must be nearly twenty."

"Bertie is not empty-headed," snapped Athena. "He is just innocent in the ways of the world."

Fuzz got a dizzy look on his face, as if he was trying really hard not to roll his eyes. "Maybe he's innocent and doesn't know his way around the world, but he knows his way around a tavern, I can tell you that. The King used to send me and a couple of castle guards to make the rounds of all the ale houses in Cogent Town, looking for Bertie. Even as a young lad of fifteen he could drink his weight in ale. We used to find him passed out on tavern floors, both his coin and his shoes missing. I used to wonder why people kept stealing his shoes. They were ghastly. Fancy leather and lace contraptions with high heels. Then I noticed that some of the women in the cheap parts of Cogent Town were wearing the exact same shoes. The pickpockets were stealing Bertie's shoes and giving them to their wives and girlfriends."

"Never mind his shoes," said Athena. "I hope you gave him a stern talking-to about how good boys do not run around to every tavern they see and guzzle all the ale."

"Nope," said Fuzz. "We just held his head under the water pump in the tavern yard until he could walk again."

"So, this Bertie," said Nikki, jumping in to prevent one of Athena's lectures on the evils of ale. "Is he friendly to the imps?"

Both Athena and Fuzz nodded.

"Yes, he has always been most generous to us," said Athena. "When my mother and Aunt Gertie came all the way from ImpHaven to visit me at Castle Cogent Bertie gave them his own chambers to stay in. He didn't even complain when Aunt Gertie accidentally hit him on the head with her cane."

"It wasn't an accident," said Fuzz. "Aunt Gertie just wanted to see if she could get away with hitting a royal. Bertie was a good sport about it. He doesn't have a lot of brains, but he's a decent chap. He spends too much on clothes and shoes, but I've seen him give a beggar woman his own velvet cloak, so I think he can be forgiven his extravagant wardrobe."

"Okay," said Nikki. "So here's my plan. I say we all go pay a visit to Gwen's mother tomorrow. You and Athena can get Bertie alone and explain to him that the imps need his help. It doesn't sound like he'll refuse."

Fuzz looked at Athena. She nodded.

"All right," said Fuzz. "Though I don't think we should all go tromping up to the Duchess of Falsa's house. Gwen can get inside with no problem. And they'll let you and Curio in because of your page uniforms. But Gwen's mother is very friendly to Rufius, and she's never been a supporter of imp rights. It could be dangerous for me and Athena to go in, so I think we should meet up somewhere else. The Duchess's house is near the Fox and Fig. It's one of the oldest taverns in Cogent Town. Huge, rambling place. You can't miss it. Gwen, see if you can convince Bertie to come out for a drink at the tavern. Shouldn't be too hard. Me and Athena will wait there for you."

Gwen nodded. "All right." She glanced down at the stained brown dress she was wearing. "Do you think you could 'borrow' something fancy for me to wear? It will put mother in a much better mood if I show up looking presentable."

"Sure," said Fuzz, yawning. "We'll swing by the market on the way. The used-clothing stalls are always full of discarded dresses. Some of the wealthier noble ladies only wear a dress once before giving it away. Now, let's all get some sleep." He gathered up the remains of the chicken and threw the carcass into the front room. Toby scrambled off the bed and dashed after it.

"I shouldn't feed him so much," said Fuzz. "If I let him go hungry he'd put more effort into catching our rat population."

"It's too bad Cation is still up at the castle," said Nikki as she crawled into the bed she was sharing with Athena. "Apparently she's Chief Mouser up there now. She's catching all kinds of rats. Did you guys bring her with you from ImpHaven?"

"Yes, Miss," said Athena, pulling the patchwork quilt up to her chin. "She cried pitifully when we tried to leave her at my mother's house. And I knew you would be missing your kitten, so I insisted we bring her. She rode in Fuzz's rucksack."

"And I have the scratches to prove it," grumbled Fuzz as he blew out the candle on the windowsill and climbed into the bed he was sharing with Curio. "Now everyone settle down and get some sleep. It's going to be a long day tomorrow."

End of Book Six

Nikki's adventures in the Realm of Reason continue in the seventh book of the *Logic to the Rescue* series.

The Logic to the Rescue series
Logic to the Rescue
The Prince of Physics
The Bard of Biology
Mystics and Medicine
The Sorcerer of the Stars
Warlock of the Wind

The Hamsters Rule series
Hamsters Rule, Gerbils Drool
Hamsters Rule the School

Excerpt from *Hamsters Rule, Gerbils Drool*

Chapter One

————◆●◆————

M ELVIN STIRRED UNEASILY in his pile of sawdust shavings. The snuffly snores coming from the twin bed across the room were disturbing his rest. He crawled out of his nest and trundled down an orange plastic tunnel to a distant corner of his Hamster Habitat. Diving head first into a pile of cedar chips, he squirmed until only his chubby rear-end was visible. He twitched for a few seconds then settled back into sleep.

Melvin should have counted himself lucky. The snores of his owner, Miss Sally Jane Hesslop, who was eleven years old as of last Tuesday, were much quieter than usual due to Sally's head being buried under her *Xena Warrior Princess* bedspread. All that could be seen of Sally was a long strand of blonde hair with a wad of pink bubble gum stuck on the end of it.

The morning sun finished clearing the fog from San Francisco bay and lit up Sally's bedroom window. The light revealed quite a mess: Legos, comic books, sneakers, mismatched socks and a spilled can of Hungry Hamster Snacks were scattered across the floor. Sally was a firm believer in keeping all of her belongings in plain view. In an emergency (and most mornings were an emergency, as Sally had a talent for being late for school) precious time could be saved by getting dressed from the clothes on the floor.

This morning Sally's peaceful slumber was destined to last only a few more brief moments, for Robbie was out of bed and on the loose.

Robbie was Sally's four-year-old brother. He was famous up and down their neighborhood for his ability to eat anything dirt-related. Mud, clay, sand, litter box filler, anything lurking in the bottom of a flowerpot or fish tank, all were fair game. When it came to dirt Robbie was an omnivore. Though, of course, he had his favorites. The light fluffiness at the heart of the vacuum cleaner bag, the tasty compost at the roots of his grandmother's roses – these were special treats for special occasions, to be savored slowly and washed down with a good quality grape Kool Aid.

Today Robbie was up at his usual time of six a.m. He tiptoed into Sally's room, a stealthy menace in his footie pajamas and bike helmet. This helmet was a permanent item in Robbie's wardrobe. Robbie was fond of banging his head on things, so his father had started putting a helmet on him as soon as Robbie got out of bed.

Giggling softly and wielding a large rubber spatula, Robbie crept up to the snoring Sally. He pulled back the edge of the bedspread with one chubby fist and brought the spatula down with a satisfying thwhack on top of Sally's head.

"Aaaah!" Sally bolted upright, her scrawny arms swinging wildly as she tried to ward off her assailant. Her oversized *Xena* T-shirt billowed out, making her eighty-pound frame look twice its size. A yellow post-it note which was stuck to her forehead fluttered in the breeze as she whipped around and grabbed the spatula from a chortling Robbie. Sally rained down a barrage of blows with the spatula onto Robbie's bike helmet. Robbie made a dash for the door, knocking over a stack of comic books. He was almost to safety, inches from escape, when he miscalculated the distance between the door jamb and his head. He bounced backwards off the door, his helmet taking most of the punishment, tripped over a half-built castle made of Legos, and toppled over onto the carpet with his feet in the air.

Sally leapt out of bed with a wild war cry and rained rubbery blows down on Robbie as if beating a stubborn batch of dough.

"Sally Jane, are you out of bed yet?" The voice floating in from the hallway sounded in desperate need of coffee. Sally's father's dearest dream was to sleep in past six a.m., a dream which was destroyed on a daily basis by Robbie and his spatula. Robbie had assigned himself the task of family alarm clock and he took his job seriously. If the first whack on the head didn't wake his target at six on the dot then Robbie would tirelessly whack until he got results. Mr. Hesslop had tried hiding the spatula in the back of the cereal cupboard, but Robbie had just switched to whacking with the toilet brush. Mr. Hesslop had quickly decided that he preferred the spatula, the toilet brush tending to catch in his hair.

Sally gave Robbie one final blow then grabbed his pajama feet and dragged him out of her room. "I'm up, Dad. I'm up," she shouted, leaving Robbie lying on his back in the hallway. Sally darted back into her room and slammed the door. She yawned, scratched her ear with the captured spatula, and surveyed her wardrobe. Her favorite pair of jeans, only slightly muddy around the knees, hung off the end of her bed. She pulled them on and selected a pink T-shirt from a pile under the window. As she pulled it over her head the post-it which was stuck to her forehead fluttered to the floor. Sally scooped it up and read it aloud.

"Charlie Sanderson must pay. Skedyul revenge for recess."

Sally's blue eyes narrowed to slits, and she smacked her palm with the spatula.

"Right. It's payday, Charlie. Today, after third period."

"OKAY, ROBBIE. YOU'VE had enough. Come and drink your juice."

Robbie, crouching over a scraggly fern which an aunt had given them for Christmas, ignored his Dad. He reached into the depths of the flowerpot and pulled up a fistful of loamy soil. He carefully picked off a ladybug which was crawling on his thumb and then crammed the dirt into his mouth.

Mr. Hesslop sighed. He grabbed Robbie off the floor and plopped him into a chair at the kitchen table. Mr. Hesslop was a taller version of Sally Jane. Both father and daughter had dishwater blond hair, blue eyes, long skinny arms and legs, and pointy elbows. Short, chubby Robbie, with his dark hair and brown eyes, looked completely unrelated to his Dad and his eleven-year-old sister, a fact which Sally mercilessly exploited. She had convinced Robbie that he was on loan from the bank that their Dad worked at, and that he could be returned at any time if she just said the word. Robbie had responded to this threat by reducing Sally's spatula wake-up calls to once a week. His Dad still got the seven-day-a-week treatment though. Robbie guessed correctly that his Dad loved him too much to pack him up and lock him in a bank vault.

"Robbie, you've got to stop eating dirt." Mr. Hesslop grabbed a paper napkin and wiped Robbie's muddy mouth. "Remember what Dr. Tompkins told you? If you don't stop you're going to have a tree growing in there." He tickled Robbie's stomach.

Robbie giggled. "Tree in tummy."

Sally wandered into the kitchen, bumping into the refrigerator. Her long, straight hair hung in front of her face like a curtain. She had attempted to braid pieces of it, and the attempt had not gone well. One braid sprouted from the top of her head like an overgrown onion. Another looked like it was growing straight out of her ear. She sat down at the kitchen table, one hand tangled in the rest of her unbraided hair, the other grabbing for a box of Cheerios.

Mr. Hesslop passed her the milk. "Sally Jane, why don't you let me help you with your hair? I'll make you look real pretty."

What could be seen of Sally's face under her hair looked suspiciously like it was rolling its eyes. "Daaad. I'm not trying to look *pretty*. I'm doing Xena braids. See, if you're in a fight you don't want your hair in your face. You can't see good."

"What fight?" Mr. Hesslop said sharply, his thin nose pointed at his daughter like a fox on the scent.

Sally smiled innocently. "I was just being hypometical, Dad. Sheesh."

"Hypothetical," said Mr. Hesslop. "Robbie, don't do that." He grabbed Robbie's juice glass, which was now half empty. Robbie had poured the rest onto the floor and was straining against his father's arm, eager to get down from the table to study (and taste) the effects of orange juice on dirty linoleum at close range.

Melvin waddled into the kitchen, his fluffy orange fur dusting a path along the un-swept floor, his nose twitching for food. He disappeared under Sally's chair, dodged her swinging feet, and settled in front of the puddle of orange juice. His tiny pink tongue darted out and lapped at lightning speed, aware that even Mr. Hesslop with his lazy housekeeping skills was unlikely to leave a bonanza like this lying around for long.

Fortunately for Melvin, Mr. Hesslop was distracted by the sound of a knock at the front door. He set Robbie down and went to greet their visitor. A few seconds later he reappeared with Darlene Trockworthy, their next-door neighbor. A peroxide blond with heavy blue eye-shadow, a too-tight dress and too-high heels, Darlene occasionally babysat Robbie and Sally. Darlene and Robbie were best friends, mainly because Darlene let Robbie eat as much dirt as he wanted, but between Darlene and Sally it had been war from the start.

Darlene slid into a seat at the kitchen table, aiming a kick at Melvin on the way. "Is that rat loose again?" she asked, her mouth full of the toast she had grabbed off of Robbie's plate.

Sally glared at her. "He's not a rat, you dingbat."

"Sally, watch your manners," Mr. Hesslop said sharply.

"Bill, the kid's rhyming again. I thought you said she'd grow out of that." Darlene pouted at Mr. Hesslop, her bright red lipstick spattered with toast crumbs. The whole neighborhood knew that Darlene had her "sights set" on Bill Hesslop, but so far he had resisted her advances.

"She'll grow out of it eventually," said Mr. Hesslop. "It's just a phase. Robbie, don't do that."

Robbie had climbed off his chair and was sitting on the floor, rubbing Cheerios in the dust on the floor before eating them.

Mr. Hesslop picked him up. "I'll clean up Mr. Dirt Devil here and drop him at his preschool. Can you take Sally?"

The look Darlene shot Sally clearly said that she'd like to dump Sally in San Francisco bay. Darlene sighed heavily. "Yeah, sure." She pointed a warning finger at Sally, a long red fingernail raking the air like a claw. "But no rhyming, kid. I mean it. One Iambic what-ya-ma-callit and I'm selling you to the slave traders. They'll ship you to Nebraska and make you shuck corn 'til you're eighty."

Sally smiled at her sweetly. "Your wish is my command. And your head is filled with sand." Sally scooped Melvin up, put him on her shoulder, and marched out of the kitchen.

"Put that rat back in his cage." Darlene yelled after her. "And if you're not ready in ten minutes I'm leaving without you."

Chapter Two

S ALLY AND DARLENE maintained a careful no-touching distance as they headed down the hill to Sally's school. When a bike rider on the sidewalk forced them to shrink the gap between them they automatically sprang apart again after the bike had passed, as if repelled by a magnetic field.

Darlene examined her makeup in a compact mirror as she tee-tered along, causing oncoming pedestrians to grumble as they jumped out of her way. Sally practiced karate kicks, viciously attacking the most dangerous looking trash cans and mailboxes along their route, her backpack flopping wildly on her shoulders.

Halfway down the hill a posse of poodles suddenly rushed out the front door of a tall apartment building and made straight for Sally. Sally threw herself down on her knees and scooped up the scruffy little white poodle which was leading the pack. The little poodle yapped excitedly, licking Sally's face. The other three poodles were tall, black, and dignified, with the fur on their heads shaped into elegant topknots. They sniffed at Sally's backpack and at Darlene's shoes. One of them lifted his leg and took aim at Darlene's stiletto. Darlene shrieked and jumped back.

"Brutus! No!"

A chubby little girl about Sally's age ran up to them and grabbed the peeing poodle. She had black curly hair and large dark eyes. She was wearing a plaid skirt, a starched white blouse, and black patent leather shoes which looked extremely uncomfortable. "Brutus, you bad dog! Sorry, Miss Trockworthy. My Mom's trying to train him not to pee on everyone, but he forgets sometimes." She herded the poodles back up the front steps of the apartment building. "C'mon Brutus, Caesar, Nero, and Fluffy. You can't come to school with us. Poodles are not allowed. Go back upstairs."

Sally waved goodbye to Fluffy and stood up, dusting off her knees. "Hi, Katie! Are you ready to rumble?"

The chubby girl looked at her in confusion. "Huh?"

Sally skipped around Katie, chanting. "Charlie's a boy, so he's not too bright. We'll shout with joy when we win this fight."

Katie picked up the book bag she had dropped during the poodle roundup. A worried frown crinkled her pale forehead. "I don't know, Sally. Remember what happened the last time you got into a fight at school? Billy Lauder's tooth got knocked out and Arnold the Iguana ate it and had to go to the Pet Hospital. I don't want Arnold to go to the Pet Hospital. He doesn't like it there. Remember the time I put my Mom's Lilac Mist hand lotion on him because he looked dry? I thought it would make him feel better, but it turned him all pink and he had to go to the Pet Hospital so they could make him green again. Arnold hates being pink. Pink is a girl's color, and Arnold's a boy iguana. Mr. Zukas says so. So you shouldn't fight."

Katie looked ready to cry. Her large eyes grew red-rimmed and shiny. Sally patted her on the shoulder and handed her a wadded up Kleenex which she pulled out of her backpack. She resumed skipping in circles.

"Arnold's not going to the Pet Hospital this time," said Sally. "I have a new Secret Revenge Plan, and there aren't any iguanas in the plan."

Katie sniffed and wiped her nose. She followed Sally and Darlene as they continued down the hill. "Oh. Well, I guess it's okay then. I'm glad Arnold isn't in your new Secret Revenge Plan, cause iguanas don't like fighting."

They reached the bottom of the hill and turned onto a narrow side street lined with gingko trees. The sidewalk was covered with fan-shaped gingko leaves. Sally swooshed at them with the toes of her sneakers, sending the leaves swirling like tiny doves. Katie carefully stepped on the bare patches of sidewalk, keeping her shiny patent leather shoes free of leaf mush. Up ahead the street was jammed with cars disgorging kids with backpacks. The kids ran into the fenced-in playground of Montgomery Elementary School, a three-story brick building with sturdy granite columns flanking its front door. The building had a basketball court on one side and a cluster of crooked pine trees on the other side.

"Okay, you two," said Darlene, finally closing her compact. "Get lost. One of your parents will pick you up after school. Don't know which parent. Don't care." She sauntered off, popping a wad of gum into her mouth. Sally stuck her tongue out at Darlene's retreating back.

"You shouldn't do that," said Katie, gasping in horror. "My Mom says that kids should always show adults the proper respect."

Sally snorted. "Darlene's not an adult. She's a doofus." She skipped around Katie, chanting. "Darlene, Darlene, she's not too keen. She's the biggest dunce you've ever seen."

Katie turned red. She quickly looked around to make sure that Darlene hadn't heard. Darlene was examining her nails as she walked away, completely oblivious to the kids dodging around her on the sidewalk. Katie breathed a sigh of relief and followed Sally into the school building.

"OKAY, EVERYONE SETTLE down!" Mr. Zukas' deep voice boomed

over the chaos in his fifth-grade classroom. He gave his sweater vest a firm tug and strode to the front of the class. "Get to your desks, pronto. Tommy, get your foot out of Kyle's mouth. Patricia, give Tiffany back her shoes. They're too small for you anyway, you clodhopper."

Thirty kids rushed to their seats with a sound like elephants tap dancing. Sally threw herself into her assigned seat in the front row of desks. Katie lowered herself demurely into the seat directly behind Sally. Arnold the Iguana calmly surveyed the classroom from his cage at the back.

Mr. Zukas opened a fat textbook. As he slowly searched for the page he wanted Sally started to fidget. She squirmed like an eel, sat on her hands, and finally couldn't contain herself any longer. She raised her arm and began waving it furiously back and forth. Mr. Zukas ignored her and turned another page.

Never one to be discouraged, Sally climbed onto her chair and waved both arms wildly like a pint-sized airport worker guiding a jumbo jet into a parking space.

"Sally Jane Hesslop," sighed Mr. Zukas, not looking up, "get down off of there before you break your neck. Not that I would mind, but the principal gets grumpy when students kick the bucket."

"Sorry, Mr. Zukas," said Sally, climbing down. "I just had a question. Can we have more discusses on evolution? Cause I looked it up on Google and a Google person says we came from tadpoles. I think it would be cool to be a tadpole. I had a tadpole once. I kept it in a Sprite bottle. After I drank the Sprite, of course. But then my brother Robbie drank the tadpole. Are we having fish sticks for lunch today?"

Mr. Zukas rubbed his forehead, looked longingly at the clock, and sighed again. "I haven't checked the lunch menu today, Sally. It's posted on the cafeteria door. You can check at recess. And no, we don't come from tadpoles. We are primates, which means we are related to the great apes. Our closest cousins are the chimpanzees. All of which I told you yesterday, and which you'd remember if you'd been paying attention. Now, class, open your history books to page thirty-four. The Pioneers. They crossed the Great Plains in covered wagons. Conditions were harsh. They had to hunt for their food."

A small red-haired boy wearing a shirt and tie waved politely from the desk next to Sally.

"Yes, Rodney?" asked Mr. Zukas. "Did you have a question?"

"Not a question, Mr. Zukas. Just a remark. It might interest the class to know that the Pioneers frequently ate deer as well as buffalo. They shot them with rifles."

Mr. Zukas beamed at him. "That's right, Rodney. I'm glad someone's been doing their homework."

Rodney smirked proudly while behind him the rest of the class rolled their eyes.

"Can anyone else tell me what other animals the Pioneers might have hunted?" asked Mr. Zukas.

Sally waved furiously.

"Anyone at all?" Mr. Zukas asked somewhat desperately.

Sally bounced up and down in her seat, arm still waving.

Mr. Zukas sighed. "Yes, Sally."

"They ate gophers."

Loud expressions of disgust erupted from the rest of the class. Sally turned around and glared at them.

"I'm fairly certain the Pioneers didn't eat gophers, Sally," said Mr. Zukas. "I believe gophers are inedible."

"Nuh-*uh*," said Sally. "Gophers are super edible. The Pioneers roasted them over campfires and put hot sauce on them. They tasted like corn dogs. Only furry."

"Eeeww." The rest of the class unanimously decided it was grossed out. Rodney cleared his throat and looked disdainfully at Sally.

"In the unlikely event that the Pioneers ate gophers," said Rodney with a sneer, "they would have skinned them first. The fur would have been removed before roasting."

"Nuh-uh," retorted Sally. "The fur's where all the vitamins are. Just like potatoes. You keep the skin on for the vitamins."

Behind Sally, Katie gasped and put her hand over her mouth. She had turned a sickly shade of green.

Mr. Zukas peered at her. "Katie, do you need to use the Little Girl's Room?"

Katie nodded tearfully at him. He waved impatiently in the direction of the door and Katie dashed out of the classroom.

Mr. Zukas sighed and turned a page in his textbook. "Let's get off the topic of the Pioneers' diet. Class, have a look at the picture on the next page. See the tin star this man is wearing? That meant he was a sheriff. He kept order in the lawless Wild West. Of course, it was a difficult job, and he needed lots of help. Frequently he would deputize. That means to create a kind of temporary sheriff. Who do you think he deputized?"

"Hamsters," said Sally at once.

Mr. Zukas pulled at his tie, looking like he was tempted to strangle himself with it. "Hamsters cannot be deputies or anything else in the law enforcement arena, Sally. Hamsters are furry rodents, just like gophers."

Sally's eyes flashed dangerously. "Hamsters are nothing like gophers! Hamsters and gophers are sworn enemies. Just ask my hamster, Melvin. You don't want to get him started on gophers. He gets so mad his fur stands straight up and he hops around like microwave popcorn. Besides, hamsters can *so* be in the law enforcement arena. Melvin is in the law enforcement arena. He's a Secret Agent. He has a Secret Agent JetPack and everything. He straps it on and flies around San Francisco looking for bad guys. If he finds any bad guys he zaps them with his Secret Agent Laser Gun." Sally jumped up and aimed an imaginary laser gun at Mr. Zukas. "Kerpow!"

Mr. Zukas sighed and put a hand on his forehead. "Recess is early today," he said. "Everyone clear out of here. And stay out until the bell rings. I don't care if a tornado sweeps through the schoolyard. If anyone so much as puts one toe inside this classroom in the next half hour I'll personally feed them to the monster that lives in the school basement. He loves to snack on little kids. Especially ones who own hamsters."

"THERE HE IS. Charlie Sanderson, Snot Extraordinaire. Are you ready?" Sally was on the Jungle Gym, hanging upside down by her knees. One of her braids had come undone and her long hair was covering her face. She parted it with her hands and peered at a blond-haired boy walking past. He was wearing baggy pants, expensive sneakers, and a backwards baseball cap and was surrounded by a bunch of boys dressed exactly like him.

Katie peered up at Sally worriedly from a safe perch on the lowest bar of the Jungle Gym. She had her skirt neatly tucked under her legs and her shiny patent leather shoes were carefully resting on a clean patch of grass. "Ready for what?" she asked.

"The Plan," whispered Sally.

"You never told me the plan. I don't know what to do. You just said you had a Secret Revenge Plan, and that there were no Iguanas."

"That's right," said Sally. "We don't need an Iguana for this plan, which is a good thing because Arnold the Iguana is retiring from the revenge business. Arnold had a little chat with Melvin at one of their Secret Agent meetings in the school cafeteria. Arnold told Melvin that he was getting too old for Secret Revenge Plans. He's going to retire to a home for elderly Iguanas in Florida. They spend all day sleeping in hammocks and drinking chocolate milkshakes. Melvin tried to talk him out of it. Mel's afraid Arnold will get fat from all the chocolate milkshakes, but Arnold's already pretty fat because Emily Nieder-

bacher keeps feeding him her peanut butter and jelly sandwiches."
Sally grabbed the Jungle Gym bar with both hands, flipped her legs
through and dropped to the ground. "We don't need Arnold for this
particular Secret Revenge Plan. You can be my back up. Follow me."

Katie sighed and reluctantly followed Sally across the playground.

Sally swerved around a group of kids playing hopscotch and sauntered in the direction of Charlie Sanderson and his posse, who were
leaning against the schoolyard's chain-link fence and attempting to
look cool. One of the boys nudged Charlie in the ribs and pointed at
Sally.

Sally walked up to Charlie and slapped him on the back. "How's
it going, Sanderson?"

The posse laughed and Charlie angrily pushed Sally away. "Get
away from me, Hesslop, you freak."

Sally smiled. "I may be a freak, but you're a geek. And may I say,
you really reek."

Charlie tried to shove her again, but Sally dodged away. She
waved at Charlie as he and his posse stalked off to a far corner of the
playground. Sally pulled something out of her pocket and tied it to the
chain-link fence.

"What are you doing?" whispered Katie. "Are we going to get in
trouble again? I can't go to the Principal's office again. I just can't.
Mrs. Finsterman always says she's going to pinch my arm with that
clothes pin she keeps on her desk."

"She won't pinch you," said Sally, watching the boys depart.

"How do you know? She always says she will."

"I know 'cause she always says she's going to pinch me too, but
she never does. It's a psychotogical strategy, like when Xena pretend-
ed to be a goddess and the Mud People worshipped her."

Katie stared at her in bafflement. "Mrs. Finsterman is a Mud
Person?"

Sally put a finger to her mouth to shush Katie and pointed at the group of boys. Charlie and his gang were about twenty yards away, torturing a first-grader by throwing pebbles at him. The first-grader hopped around like a frightened puppy, not sure whether to cry or run.

Sally checked the fence and muttered to herself. "Two more feet. Come on, you poophead. Keep walking."

Katie frowned at her in confusion. She peered at the group of boys then bent down to examine the fence. "Sally, what . . ."

Sally waved her arms to shush her. The school bell rang, signaling the end of recess. Kids started running for the doors. Charlie Sanderson and his posse followed at a leisurely pace. Suddenly Charlie halted, frowning. He pulled at the waistline of his baggy pants, shrugged, and took another step. Sally yanked Katie away from the fence, giggling wildly. She ran into the school building, pulling Katie along behind her.

A huge burst of laughter suddenly erupted from the school yard. Sally stood on her tiptoes and peeked out of the glass window in the front door of the building. Charlie Sanderson was standing in the middle of the playground with his baggy pants down around his ankles and his *Finding Nemo* underpants on display for all to see. Kids pointed at him, wetting themselves from laughing. Grinning wickedly, Sally pulled a small piece of fishing line from her pocket and showed it to Katie.

Chapter Three

S ALLY WAS LYING on the floor of the Hesslop's living room, peering under an armchair. Muttering under her breath, she reached under the chair and pulled out a slinky and a blackened banana peel. Behind her, Robbie was sitting in the middle of the room wearing Snoopy underpants and his bike helmet. He giggled and whacked himself on the head with a toilet brush, matching the rhythm of Michael Jackson's *Beat it*, which was playing on the radio.

Sally sighed. The armchair was not delivering the goods. She crawled over to the sofa. Darlene Trockworthy was sitting there with her legs stretched out on the coffee table, painting her toenails. As she crawled under Darlene's legs Sally accidentally bumped them. A streak of Cotton Candy pink shot across Darlene's toes and up her ankle.

"Damn it, kid," groused Darlene, "Watch what you're doing. You made me mess up my pedicure."

"Sorry," Sally mumbled grudgingly. "It's just that I can't find Melvin. Have you seen him?"

"Nope, and good riddance," said Darlene. "That rodent's always creeping around underfoot. I swear he tries to trip me on purpose."

Sally sat back on her heels and smirked at Darlene. "He does that 'cause it's part of his Secret Mission. He's Special Agent Melvin, and he goes to Washington BC every weekend for Super Secret Hamster Orders. He's trained to trip all enemy combatants."

Darlene wiped the nail polish off her foot. "Well, if you can't find him maybe he's at the White House meeting the President," she said. "I hear they serve hamster every Friday."

Sally gave her an evil glare and flopped on her stomach to peer under the sofa.

Behind her Melvin suddenly appeared, rolling across the living room on an old-fashioned four-wheeled roller skate. His chubby rear-end didn't quite fit on the skate, and he dusted a path across the floor with his fur. He rolled from one end of the room to the other and disappeared into the kitchen. Robbie waved the toilet brush at him as he passed.

Sally pulled her head out from under the sofa and hopped to her feet. She planted her fists on her hips. "Drat you, Melvin. Where *are* you? If you're hiding in the microwave again I'm going to spank your little furry butt. You know Dad hates it when his microwave popcorn tastes like hamster."

She stomped into the kitchen and opened the microwave. No Melvin. She banged open cupboards and rattled pans. "Melvin, if you've gone on a Secret Mission again you are soooo in trouble. You know you aren't supposed to go on Secret Missions after your bedtime. I'm gonna write to Washington. They'll remote you back to Janitor Melvin and take away your Secret Agent Jetpack."

Sally crawled under the kitchen table and peered inside an empty box of Wheaties. Behind her Melvin had managed (by methods known only to himself and other Secret Agent Hamsters) to get himself on top of the fridge. He poked his nose over the side and surveyed the perilous drop to the kitchen counter. After a moment's hesitation, he stepped off the fridge, executing a perfect swan dive with a half-twist. He landed face-first on the kitchen counter then slowly toppled over onto his back, legs in the air. He tried to roll onto his feet but was hampered by a touch of middle-aged spread. After several tries he got himself right-side up and waddled to the edge of the countertop. At that moment Robbie wandered in, fencing with his toilet brush. Melvin took a step into the unknown and landed splat on top of Robbie's bike helmet, all four feet splayed out and hanging on for dear life. Oblivious to his stowaway, Robbie fenced back into the living room, taking Melvin with him.

"Sally, get off the floor," said Mr. Hesslop as he entered the kitchen, a pencil behind his ear and the grumpy look of a man who's just been wrestling with his tax returns. "You're as bad as Robbie. Remember, you're supposed to set a good example for him. Now, go brush your teeth. It's bedtime."

Sally scrambled out from under the table and saluted. "Sir. Yes Sir. Your orders we obey. We're here to save the day. Good dental hygiene is a must. We'll clean our teeth or bust." She marched out of the kitchen, humming a martial tune. At the end of the hall she pivoted sharply and entered a small bathroom whose plumbing fixtures dated from the fifties. A bulging hamper full of wet towels sat in the corner and a flotilla of rubber ducks was lined up along the edge of the bathtub. The back of the toilet overflowed with half-empty shampoo bottles.

Sally knelt and began throwing towels out of the hamper. "Melvin, you varmint, you're about to become a garment. My Xena doll needs a fur coat, and you've got my vote."

She stuck her head into the now empty hamper. Behind her Melvin sauntered into the bathroom and scrambled up onto the edge of the tub, climbing the pyramid of wet towels Sally had dumped on the floor. He wound his way along the rim of the bathtub, which was full of soapy water leftover from Robbie's bath. Melvin dodged the rubber ducks with surprising agility, but overconfidence got the better of him and he slipped, falling into the bathtub with a splash.

Sally pulled her head out of the hamper and rushed over. "Melvin, you poophead. Your Secret Agent Swimming Lessons aren't til next week."

A stream of bubbles floating up from under the water was the only answer. Sally scooped Melvin up and deposited him on the bathroom rug. Melvin shook like a tiny dog and sat shivering, his orange fur matted to his sides.

"It's okay, Mel," said Sally. "I'll fix you right up with my Top Secret Air Blaster."

She grabbed a blow drier and turned it on High. The blast of hot air rolled Melvin over backward. He did a full somersault and ended up on standing on his head against the side of the bathtub. Sally picked him up and aimed the blow drier at his tummy. His fur blew straight backward as if he was in a hurricane. When Sally had finished drying him he was twice his normal size and had the hamster version of an Afro.

"Melvin! That's a great disguise. You can use it on your next undercover mission. Nobody will ever recognize you. You can be Horace the Hairdresser, famous for your skills with a curling iron. All the lady hamsters will be lining up to make an appointment with you."

Melvin's Afro started to deflate.

"Hang on Melvin," said Sally. "You just need some Product to maintain volume. That's what those hair commercials on TV are always saying."

Sally grabbed a can of hair mousse from the cabinet under the sink and sprayed a big glob on Melvin, who promptly disappeared under a pile of foam. Sally dug him out of the foam and rubbed the mousse into his fur, then snatched a toothbrush from the sink. "This is Dad's. He won't mind," said Sally as she brushed Melvin's fur into spikes. She sat him back down on the bathroom rug.

"There! You totally look like a cool dude. You look like one of those singers on American Idol. You just need to learn how to dance."

Sally jumped up and launched into a wild dance step. Melvin backed into a corner as Sally's flailing arms whacked the shower curtain and knocked a shampoo bottle into the toilet. Sally finished with a flourish and bowed low before an imaginary audience. "C'mon Mel. It's not hard. You just do little wiggle and a little rap. You just gotta have attitude. Like this."

Sally grabbed a rubber duck and sang into it like a microphone. "My name's Sally J. and I'm here to say, I'm doing my dance 'cause I pulled down Charlie's pants."

Sally picked up Melvin and danced around with him. "You need a hamster rap. All the tough hamsters have one. And maybe some bling. I wonder if Dad would buy you a gold chain."

Melvin looked decidedly skeptical about this, not to mention sea-sick from all the dancing.

Sally danced into her bedroom, singing. "I'm furry and I'm cute. I'm a Secret Agent to boot. I've got a special JetPack which is totally wack."

She tucked Melvin into his Hamster Habitat. Melvin trundled down the orange tube to his usual nest, his sticky moussed fur attracting bits of sawdust. By the time he reached his nest in the middle of the Habitat he looked like a tiny pile of kindling.

"Another super disguise, Mel," said Sally. "Totally cool. You can do your next Secret Mission at Tony's Pizza. They have sawdust all over their floor. They'll never spot you. You can sneak into the kitchen and find out the ingredients of their Secret Pizza Sauce."

Melvin burrowed into the sawdust of his nest until he was just a sawdust-lump. Sally yawned and blew him a kiss. "Night Mel."

Chapter Four

"**S**ALLY JANE HESSLOP, you are a demon spawn."

Mrs. Patterson, leader of Brownie Troop 112, wiped the milk off her sour face and glared down at Sally. The two of them were faced off in the middle of the Montgomery Elementary School cafeteria. A table with cartons of milk and a plate of Rice Krispie Treats was setup in one corner.

The wayward milk had ended up on Mrs. Patterson's face through totally unavoidable circumstances. Sally had been chasing another Brownie while holding a carton of milk and a straw. Squirting had been inevitable.

Sally planted her fists on her hips and regaled Mrs. Patterson with a cold stare. They were old enemies. They had disliked each other from the very first day that Mrs. Patterson had assumed the leadership of the troop. On that fateful day Sally had been showing the other brownies how to slide along the newly polished wooden floor in their stocking feet. She had just launched into a particularly energetic slide when Mrs. Patterson had walked through the door of the cafeteria. The resulting collision had knocked Mrs. Patterson off her feet and onto her support-hose covered knees. Mrs. Patterson had been trying to transfer Sally to another Brownie troop ever since, so far without success.

"Well," said Sally, "if I'm a demon spawn then I bet it's a cool demon, one that can shoot flames out of its eyeballs. I wish I could shoot flames out of my eyeballs. I'd turn Charlie Sanderson into a crispy critter."

Mrs. Patterson raised her eyes to the heavens. "When I say that you are a demon spawn, Sally Jane Hesslop, it means that you are a very bad girl. One of the worst I've had the misfortune to meet in all my years of guiding Brownies along the difficult path to becoming young ladies."

Sally fiddled with her straw. "I'd rather be a demon spawn than a young lady. I bet demon spawn have cool super powers. The coolest super power would be to turn people into potato bugs. My first victim would be Charlie Sanderson. If I turned him into a potato bug it would be a big improvement. I'd probably get a medal from the President. Then they'd have a parade for me and I'd ride on a float past the White House and wave to the crowd. Like this." Sally energetically waved her arms, spraying drops of milk onto Mrs. Patterson's bouffant hairdo.

Mrs. Patterson closed her eyes and kneaded her forehead with two shaking fingers. "Sally Jane Hesslop, we were discussing you spewing milk everywhere and making a mess, not super powers and potato bugs. Now go get some paper towels from the restroom and wipe this up."

"Okay" said Sally, shrugging. She tucked the straw under her Brownie beanie. "When do we get to make bird feeders from pinecones? That's in the Brownie handbook, you know. Page forty-nine. You stick peanut butter in the pinecones so the birds can peck it out. Though I don't understand why we can't just spread the peanut butter on Ritz crackers. Then the birds could peck it real easy. Molly Sanderson says it's because the birds like to work hard for their food, but that's just stupid. Besides, Molly is Charlie Sanderson's sister and she picks her nose, so you know anything she says is suspected. That's what my Dad says. Nose pickers are Dim Bulbs and to be suspected. The crackers don't have to be Ritz. Wheat Thins would work good too."

Mrs. Patterson sighed. "Sally Jane Hesslop, I don't know what you're blathering on about. Get this mess cleaned up. *Now.*"

Mindy Nichols, a thin black girl with red bows on the ends of her cornrows, ran up to Sally. She peered after the departing Mrs. Patterson with a fearful expression. "Sally, guess what? Mrs. Osterman isn't coming today. She's in the hospital."

Mrs. Osterman was the co-leader of the troop. She was a quiet young woman with a warm smile who was liked by all the Brownies.

"You mean it's just us and Prissy Patterson?" groaned Sally. "Oh barf. Why is Mrs. Osterman in the hospital?"

"Molly Sanderson says it's because she's having an *operation*," whispered Mindy.

Sally rolled her eyes. "Molly is always saying stupid stuff. You know that. She's a Sanderson. You can't believe anything she says. C'mon. Let's go ask Sandra Chang. She'll know."

Sally and Mindy ran up to a group of girls gathered around Sandra Chang, a tall, graceful Chinese girl with a curtain of shiny black hair hanging all the way to her hips. A purple silk scarf was artfully tied around the neck of her Brownie uniform.

Sally barged her way through the group. "Hey Sandra."

Sandra nodded at her graciously, like a benevolent Queen acknowledging her subjects.

"Sandra, what's up with Mrs. Osterman? Mindy says she's in the hospital."

"I'm sorry, Sally," replied Sandra Chang in a quiet, authoritative voice. "I don't know the details. All I know is that Mrs. Patterson is taking over as Troop Leader."

Loud groans erupted from all the Brownies within earshot. Molly Sanderson, a short, pudgy blond girl with two front teeth missing, sister to the infamous Charlie Sanderson, jumped up and down frantically, waving her hand as if in school.

"Thandra. Thandra," lisped Molly, "I know what'th happened to Mrs. Othterman. My brother Charlie told me."

On hearing Charlie's name Sally made loud gagging noises and clutched her throat. Molly ignored her, looking intently at Sandra. Finally Sandra gave her a regal nod.

"Mrs. Othterman ith having a Hystertology," whispered Molly excitedly. "That'th an operation. It meanth thee can't have babiesth anymore, unlesth she goeth to Mexico and getsth it reverthed. Then her babiesth will come out backwardsth, like when your Dad backth the car out of the garage. Latht week my Dad backed our car out of the garage and ran over my brother'th bicycle. My Dad said a very bad wordth."

Sally planted her hands on her hips and gave Molly a look of scathing contempt. "That's not a Hystertology, Sanderson. A Hystertology is when you have your ears pinned back. The doctor staples them to your head so you don't look like Dumbo."

"Mrs. Othterman doesthn't look like Dumbo," said Molly.

"Well, not anymore," shot back Sally. "She's had a Hystertology. Sheesh, Sanderson. You are such a dimwit sometimes. I guess it runs in the family."

Molly advanced on her, fists clenched. "You take that back Hessthlop."

Sally assumed a Xena fighting pose. "C'mon, Sanderson. I'll lick you, and then I'll go lick your stupid brother."

"Charlie's a twit,

He's Molly's brother.

He has half a wit,

Molly has the other."

Sally raised her leg in preparation for a super-duper martial arts kick. Molly stood her ground for a second, then thought better of it and dashed off to find Mrs. Patterson.

"Girls! Girls!" shouted Mrs. Patterson from the center of the cafeteria. "Everyone gather round. It's Share Time. Bring the item you're going to share with the group over here."

There was a noisy scramble as all the Brownies rushed to a pile of backpacks stacked against the wall, and then convened in the center of the room. They threw themselves on the wooden floor in a cross-legged circle around Mrs. Patterson.

"Molly, dear, why don't you go first," said Mrs. Patterson.

Molly Sanderson smirked at the others and walked to the center of the circle. She held up a Barbie doll dressed in an immaculate princess-type costume of white silk with a red velvet cape. "Thith ith Princeth Thophie of Bavaria. Thee's dressthed for the ball. Thee's a Spethial Edition. My Mom bought her for me in New York at Bloomingdaleth."

"She's just beautiful, Molly," said Mrs. Patterson. "So precious. I bet all the young ladies here want to be Princesses, don't you, girls?"

Sally sprang up. "Of course. I'm Princess Scary Fighting Eagle from the Moping Moose tribe. We get dressed for balls too. We paint our faces with red stripes, stick eagle feathers in our ears, and do our Special Moose Waltz around the campfire."

Sally launched into a fast-paced dance, shaking her arms and kicking her legs over her head. Her Brownie beanie flew off, and girls scrambled backwards as she lunged wildly toward them. She concluded by spinning rapidly in a circle, then staggered dizzily back to her spot on the floor.

Mrs. Patterson closed her eyes during this performance. After Sally had sat down again she opened her eyes, a pained expression on her face. "Mindy," she sighed, "why don't you go next?"

Mindy Nichols moved to the center of the circle, bashfully pulling at her cornrows. She pulled a brightly colored paper bird from a bag. Several of the Brownies oohed and aahed. Mindy smiled gratefully. "This is a Japanese art called Origami. My Mom learned it when she was stationed at a Navy base in Sasebo, Japan. She taught it to me. This is a tsuru. That's Japanese for crane. All the kids in Japan learn to make them. The crane is a symbol of peace." Mindy sat down abruptly, looking embarrassed. The Brownies applauded.

Mrs. Patterson pursed her lips as if she'd just drunk lemon juice. "Very, er, multi-cultural, Mindy. Though maybe you should bring something a little more American next time. These exotic things aren't really Brownie appropriate for Brownie meetings. Let's see, Sandra, why don't you come up."

Sandra Chang nodded and rose gracefully to her feet. She unrolled a paper scroll which displayed a vertical line of beautiful Chinese characters. "This is called calligraphy. It's a very popular art in China. These characters are in the Mandarin language, which my mother and grandmother speak. My grandmother taught me how to do calligraphy. We use a pot of black ink and a brush made of sheep's hair."

Sandra sat down and the Brownies applauded respectfully.

"My goodness," said Mrs. Patterson, "This is certainly an international group. I feel like I'm at the United Nations. Well, onward. Who'd like to volunteer?"

Sally waved her arm wildly. Another Brownie across from Sally dared to raise her arm as well. Sally glared daggers at her opponent, and the offending Brownie promptly dropped her challenge and looked like she'd be thrilled to sink into the floor. Mrs. Patterson tried mightily to avoid Sally's gaze, but resistance was futile. Sally marched unbidden to the center of the circle, carrying a paper takeout carton. Mrs. Patterson raised her eyes heavenward.

"I'll go next, Mrs. Patterson," said Sally. She opened the carton and pulled out something wriggly. The Brownies gasped in horror and the ones closest scooted away. Molly Sanderson screamed.

"Mrsth. Patterthon, Thally'th brought a rat! Eeeuww. Make her take ith away!"

Sally rolled her eyes. "It's not a rat, Sanderson, you doofus. It's my hamster, Melvin. My Dad shaved him. See, what happened was, I put some of Darlene Trockworthy's Super Hold Hair Mousse on him. Darlene wants to be my Dad's girlfriend, and she left her hair mousse in our bathroom."

Mrs. Patterson clutched the pearls around her neck and muttered something about tramps.

"Anyway," continued Sally, "it turns out you should never mousse a hamster. It glues their fur up something awful. Plus you should especially never put mousse on your hamster and then let him roll around in sawdust. My Dad said there must have been some kind of chemical reaction between the pine sap in the sawdust and Darlene's Super Hold Hair Mousse. It hardened up like that shellac stuff we used on our birdhouses last year. Poor Mel here couldn't even walk. He just rolled around like a pinecone with feet. So my Dad used his electric razor and shaved off all of Melvin's fur. So now Mel's got a crew cut, like an Army guy. Anybody want to hold him?"

The Brownies all recoiled. Melvin dove back into the takeout container as Mrs. Patterson stepped forward and made shooing motions at Sally. Sally reluctantly relinquished center stage and sat back down. She dropped a Rice Krispie Treat into the takeout carton. "It's okay, Mel," she whispered into the carton, "Don't mind Prissy Patterson. The troop loved you. You were a big hit."

Chapter Five

"I WISH YOU could have been there, Katie. Melvin was the star of the show. It was like American Idol, but with hamsters."

Sally and Katie were walking across a wide green lawn. Sally was wearing baggy blue shorts and a T-shirt that said "Girl Power!" in sparkly red and blue letters. On her feet she had one red basketball sneaker and one black one. Katie was uncomfortably over-dressed, as usual, in a starched white blouse with a Peter Pan collar, a kilt, and black patent-leather Mary Janes. Sally was swinging a takeout container by its wire handle.

"American what?" asked Katie.

"Oh jeez Katie. Are your parents *ever* going to let you watch TV?"

"Probably not. They say it turns your brain into Swiss Cheese."

"That's just stupid," said Sally. "Everyone knows that brains are made out of spaghetti. Don't you remember Mindy's Halloween party? We had to put our hands in the brains, and they were spaghetti. Cooked spaghetti, of course. Nobody has raw spaghetti for brains, except maybe Charlie Sanderson. Hey, want to see Melvin's outfit?"

She stopped and set the takeout container down on the grass. When she opened it Melvin popped his head out, his whiskers twitching. He was wearing a purple and white striped doggie sweater. Sally picked him up and held him out to Katie, who scratched his shaved head. Melvin yawned and had a good stretch, waving his tiny tail back and forth, which was the only part of him which still had fur on it. Sally put him on her shoulder. "Isn't this sweater cute? Mel was cold without his fur, so my Dad bought it at a pet store. They didn't have any hamster sweaters, so he got this one. It's for Chihuahua puppies. Melvin didn't want to wear kid's clothes, but I finally talked him into it."

"It's very stylish," said Katie.

"You bet," said Sally, scratching Melvin's nose. "Mel's a stylin' dude. I wish you could have been at our Brownie meeting. We had Show and Tell. Sandra Chang brought some fancy writing called colonoscopy, cause she's Chinese. Mindy Nichols brought this paper bird called a guru. You could have brought that droodle toy. I don't get why your parents hate the Brownies."

"It's a dreidel, not a droodle. And my parents don't hate the Brownies. They just don't like Mrs. Patterson. They don't like the way she's always telling people they aren't American."

"Yeah, she's stuck on that," said Sally. "My Dad says she's got a psychotological problem about it. A Pixation. That's when Pixies get inside your head and turn your brain into scrambled eggs. Hey, if Mrs. Patterson watches a lot of TV and your parents are right about the Swiss Cheese, then her brain will turn into a cheese omelet."

They passed through a garden full of pink and yellow roses. In front of them loomed an imposing mansion flanked by towering oak trees. A driveway bordered with rhododendrons led to the front entrance, but Sally headed toward a door on the side of the house.

Katie glanced around nervously. "Gosh, this is a very fancy house. Is your grandma nice?" she asked, her voice shaking.

"Oh yeah," said Sally. "She's super nice. Well, to me, anyway. She's only mean to people she doesn't like. Like salespeople and missionaries. She chases them. Once she chased this missionary all the way down the driveway. She was hitting him on the head with a broom. She said she wanted to hit him on the head with a shovel, but then she'd have to hide the body. Bodies are hard to hide. They turn into zombies and start showing up every day for breakfast. And my grandma *hates* having guests for breakfast. She always has her breakfast in bed. A piece of toast with two poached eggs and her special coffee. I tasted her special coffee once. It made me hiccup. My Dad took it away and said I was too young for special coffee."

Katie started to whimper quietly. "What if she doesn't like *me?*"

Sally patted her on the shoulder. "Don't worry, Katie. I promise she'll like you. It's just salespeople, missionaries, and Mean Darlene Trockworthy she doesn't like. Grandma says Darlene is on the make. That means she wears too much makeup. Which is *sooo* true. Once I saw a huge piece of her face fall off. It just peeled off like a big piece of paint peeling off a wall. It was *so* gross."

Katie turned a bit green around the gills. She took an embroidered handkerchief out of the pocket of her kilt and coughed into it. Sally went up to the side of the house and stood on tiptoe to peer in a window. Robbie was inside the house. All that could be seen of him was his rear-end, which was hanging over the edge of a large pot full of daisies. Sally pushed open the side door.

"C'mon, Katie," said Sally. "It'll be fine, you'll see."

Sally skipped into the room and grabbed hold of Robbie's shorts, hauling him out of the flowerpot. Robbie was wearing a little sailor suit and tennis shoes. A goatee of dirt circled his mouth. Sally sighed and shook her head. Robbie grinned at her and held up a worm in his chubby little fist. Sally grabbed it a split second before he put it in his mouth. She deposited the worm back into the flowerpot.

"Katie, can I borrow your handkerchief?"

Katie looked at her, then down at Robbie. She reluctantly pulled out her lacy handkerchief and handed it over. Sally scrubbed Robbie's face with it until his face turned red and the handkerchief turned brown. Robbie giggled and ran off, pulling another worm out of the pocket of his sailor suit.

"C'mon," said Sally. "Just follow Robbie. He's probably headed straight for grandma. She always stuffs him with sugar cookies. They're his favorite. After dirt, of course. And dust bunnies. He's been on a dust bunny binge lately. Yesterday my Dad found him under his bed, rolling the dust bunnies into little pancakes and pouring maple syrup on them."

Sally and Katie ran after Robbie, who led them down a hallway lined with beautiful silk wallpaper. Robbie ran his hand along the wallpaper, leaving a long brown streak of dirt. At the end of the hall he darted out of a sliding glass door.

When Sally and Katie followed Robbie through the door they found themselves on a patio which had a spectacular view of San Francisco bay and the Golden Gate Bridge.

Bill Hesslop, dressed in a suit and tie, was perched on the edge of a deckchair. Next to him, stretched out comfortably on a matching chair, was Sally's grandmother. Mrs. Belinda Worthington was a trim, stylish woman of sixty-five with white hair and blue eyes. She wore tailored trousers and a cashmere sweater. Robbie ran up to her, pulling something out of the pocket of his sailor suit.

Mrs. Worthington held out her hand. "What have you got there, Mr. Robert?"

Robbie deposited a large pink earthworm into her hand. Bill Hesslop winced, but Mrs. Worthington didn't even blink. "Well. This is a fine big wriggler, isn't he? It's too bad your grandpa isn't with us anymore. He'd take this fine specimen down to the pond and show you how to catch a fish with him. The gardener stocks the pond with trout, you know."

Robbie nodded at her solemnly. "Fishes eat worms." Robbie took the worm back and tried to put it in his mouth, but his grandmother was too quick for him. She calmly snatched up the worm and handed it to Bill Hesslop. "Bill, dear. Dispose of this, would you."

"Yes, ma'am." He sighed and carried the worm down to the lawn. Sally ran up to Mrs. Worthington and gave her a hug. "Hi, grandma! Look who I brought! This is my best friend, Katie Greenwald. Just so you know, Katie's not a salesperson or a missionary. She's a fifth-grader. We're in the same class at school."

Sally waved at Katie to come nearer, but Katie shook her head vigorously, looking terrified.

Mrs. Worthington smiled at her. She picked up a plate of cookies from a small table next to her deckchair. "Katie, I can tell by your tasteful outfit that you are a young lady of distinction. Now, I have here some wonderfully refined Petit Fours which I'm sure will appeal to your palate. Come try one."

Katie shyly approached and took a cookie. "It's very nice, ma'am."

"Such lovely manners," said Mrs. Worthington. "You could learn a thing or two from your friend, Miss Sally."

Sally tried to swallow the cookie she'd grabbed and stuffed into her mouth. "I have super good manners," she said, her voice muffled by cookie. "You told me so last time I was here, grandma. You said my compartments were spotless."

"Your comportment, dear. Your comportment was spotless. It means you were behaving like a little lady during that visit. Quite out of character, it was. You must have been ill. Perhaps a touch of flu. Usually you dash about like a little wombat that's gotten into my diet pills."

"What's a wombat?" asked Sally, taking another cookie.

"A small creature, dear. Very hyperactive. Speaking of small creatures, where is that animal you're always carting around? I hope he isn't loose in the house. Last time you were here Cook found him in the pantry. He popped out at her from behind a jar of pickled beets. She came running to me, screaming something about mice and threatening to quit. It took a bottle of my best brandy to calm her down."

"Melvin's right here, grandma. See?" Sally pointed at her shoulder, but Melvin wasn't there. Sally lifted her hair and felt around the back of her neck. No Melvin.

Her grandmother gave her a suspicious look. "Sally Jane Hesslop. Is that miniature marauder loose in my house again?"

"No, no," said Sally hurriedly. "Everything's fine, grandma. I put Melvin in a safe place, where he wouldn't bother anybody. I'll just go check on him." She made shooing motions at Katie, who backed nervously towards the house. Sally walked nonchalantly to the door, then yanked it open and pushed Katie through.

"Dang that Melvin," Sally grouched as she dashed down the hall. "He must have jumped ship and gone exploring. C'mon, Katie. We have to find him before Mrs. Beatty does. That's grandma's cook. She makes the best fudge brownies in the world, and grandma's always saying she loves Mrs. Beatty's cooking better than she loves her own family. Grandma'll be really mad if Mrs. Beatty leaves on account of Melvin."

Katie puffed along behind Sally. "Why does Mrs. Beatty hate Melvin?" she asked breathlessly. "He's a nice hamster. Even my Mom likes him. Remember that time you brought him over to our apartment? My Mom said he was a prince among gerbils."

"Well, of course he's a prince among gerbils," said Sally. "Hamsters are way, way better than stinky old gerbils. Mrs. Beatty's problem is she can't tell that Melvin's a hamster. She thinks he's a mouse. Every time she sees him she tries to hit him with her rolling pin."

Katie gasped in horror.

Sally sang a tune as she ran:

"Mel, I know you're in the house.

Mrs. Beatty thinks you're a mouse.

Come out before you get bashed.

Hamsters look better un-smashed."

Suddenly a loud scream echoed through the house. "Shoot!" said Sally. "That's Mrs. Beatty. C'mon!"

They rushed into the kitchen, where Mrs. Beatty was standing near the oven wearing her usual uniform of flower-print dress, hairnet, and apron. Interrupted in the middle of her daily baking, she was eyeing a mixing bowl and waving a rolling pin at it. She took a step towards the bowl as it rattled. Whiskers poked over the edge, then slid back down. When they appeared again, the flour-covered head of Melvin could be seen peering over the edge of the bowl.

Melvin squirmed and wriggled and managed to pull himself up onto the rim of the bowl. It tottered and tipped over, spilling Melvin and a cascade of flour onto the kitchen counter.

Mrs. Beatty let out a war whoop and brought the rolling pin crashing down onto the counter. She missed Melvin by a whisker. He scrambled along the flour-dusted countertop, dashed around a carton of eggs, and dove head first into the open maw of a food processor. Mrs. Beatty yelled in triumph and leapt forward. She hit the 'On' switch of the food processor.

The processor began to spin, taking Melvin with it. He went around, faster and faster. Just as he was in danger of becoming hamster McNuggets he was flung out of the food processor. He flew through the air and landed face first in a bowl full of walnuts, scattering nuts everywhere.

The walnuts shifted under his feet as Melvin frantically sped up, trying to scramble out of the bowl. Nuts started flying through the air like tiny cannonballs, pelting Mrs. Beatty in the face. She raised her rolling pin and warded them off like a Jedi master blocking bullets with his light saber.

Mrs. Beatty hit a walnut through the open kitchen window, clobbering a pigeon which was flying across the lawn. It squawked and crash-landed on the grass. Ducking walnuts, Sally grabbed Melvin and jumped back out of range of Mrs. Beatty's rolling pin. Melvin shook himself, showering Sally in flour. "Jeez, Mel," said Sally. "What a mess. You need a bath. You look like a dumpling with feet."

"A bath!" yelled Mrs. Beatty, shaking her rolling pin. "Do not talk to me of baths! What is needed is a mousetrap with a nice strong spring. Snap!" She whacked her rolling pin down on the counter with a bang.

Sally and Katie jumped. "C'mon, Mrs. Beatty," said Sally. "You don't really mean that. Melvin's very sorry he disturbed your cooking. Aren't you, Mel?" Sally held Melvin up to her eyes and glared at him.

Melvin stared back at her and yawned. He was clearly not in an apologetic mood, rolling pin or no rolling pin.

Mrs. Beatty snorted and shook the rolling pin at them. "Out of my kitchen! All of you! I am making croque en bouche. It is a very delicate process, not to be interrupted by small children and mice! Out!"

Sally, Katie, and Melvin beat a hasty retreat.

"I BET THEY'VE gone down to the stables," said Sally, surveying the empty patio. Her father, grandmother, and Robbie were nowhere to be seen. A lone sparrow pecked at the crumbs of the Petit Fours. "C'mon, maybe grandma'll let us ride Max!" She dashed down the steps of the patio two at a time and headed across the lawn.

"Who's Max?" Katie asked, breath coming in gasps as she tried to keep up.

"He's a Shetland pony," said Sally, slowing down so Katie could catch up. "He's super gentle. You can ride on his back without a saddle. Plus he's got long blond hair called a mane. Grandma lets me brush it. When it's brushed Max looks just like a princess. Well, he would if he weren't a horse. Or a boy."

"I don't know if I want to meet Max," Katie said dubiously. "I think I might be afraid of horses."

"What do you mean, 'might' be? Don't you know?"

"I'm not sure," said Katie. "I've never seen a horse, not in person I mean."

Sally changed course and headed for a birdbath in the center of the lawn. "You have *so* seen a horse. Remember that policeman who yelled at us just cause we were climbing that lamppost? He was riding a horse."

"He was yelling at *you*, not me," said Katie. "*I* wasn't climbing the lamppost. I was holding your backpack and Melvin. Melvin didn't want to climb the lamppost either. And the horse was way over across the street. If the horse had been on our side of the street I'm pretty sure I would have been afraid of it."

"Well, you won't be afraid of Max. And anyway, he's a pony, not a horse. Ponies are kinda like horses that have shrunk. You know, like that time my Dad wasn't home and I did the laundry all by myself and all of my Dad's sweaters shrank. It was weird. They came out of the dryer looking like little kids clothes. Robbie wears them now. Your Mom's got some nice sweaters. I specially like that pink fuzzy one. If you ever want some new clothes, just do the laundry." Sally stopped at the birdbath. It had moss growing along its sides and was full of rainwater. A sparrow was perched on the rim, watching them warily. "Okay, Mel. It's bath time."

She lowered Melvin into the water. When she let go he promptly sank down to the moldy bottom of the birdbath. Sally grabbed him off the bottom and swished him around in the water, leaving a trail of flour floating like dust on the water's surface.

"There you go, Mel. Much better. Though I can see you're overdue for your Secret Agent swimming lessons. You might want to sign up next time you're in Washington BC. And make sure you use Water

Wings the first time. Katie uses them."

"Oh, yes", said Katie, nodding enthusiastically. "Definitely use Water Wings, Melvin. One time, Charlie Sanderson pushed me into the pool at Rimrock Park when I wasn't wearing my Water Wings. The lifeguard had to pull me out and hit my back to get all the water out. I had pool water in my tummy for days afterward. You could hear it splashing around when I walked."

Melvin regarded her with appropriate solemnity upon hearing this information.

Sally pulled off Melvin's wet sweater and set him on her shoulder. "I hope he doesn't catch cold. Melvin's very delicate. And sensitive. My Dad says he's an old soul. That means he's a good listener. He knows all kinds of super-secret stuff, but he never tells anyone. That would be against the Super Secret Hamster Code of Rules and Regulations. Nope, if you've got a secret, tell a hamster."

"Gerbils are verbal

And sip tea that is herbal.

They gossip and chat

About this and that.

So if you've got secrets to tell,

A hamster is swell.

Do what you will,

They'll never spill."

Sally and Katie (and Melvin, shivering on Sally's shoulder and dripping water down the back of her t-shirt) followed a stone-covered path which led from the lawn into a grove of birch trees. A patch of bluebells clustered under the waving trees. Sally picked one of the tiny flowers and held it up for Melvin to sniff. He nosed it warily and then suddenly swallowed it, causing hamster convulsions as he choked on the petals. To prevent himself from falling off Sally's shoulder Melvin dug his claws into her T-shirt.

"Ouch! Dang it Melvin, that hurt." Sally detached him from her T-shirt and held him up at eye level. "What do you say? Hmm?"

Melvin was not known for his expressiveness, but it did appear that his whiskers had a hint of apology about them.

"That's right," said Sally. "You say you're sorry. Grandma's always saying how I need some etiquette lessons. Maybe you should have some too. You can't be a Secret Agent if you don't have good etiquette."

"What's etiquette?" asked Katie.

"It's these rules on how to behave in all situations. Like, if you burp really loudly at a fancy dinner party you should point to the person next to you. Hamsters know all these rules automatically, but I think maybe Melvin needs a refresher course."

Up ahead the trees thinned out and the path they were on ended at a white-fenced corral. Mrs. Worthington was mounted on a chestnut mare, putting the glossy-coated horse through its paces. Together horse and rider turned and spun expertly around the corral. Mrs. Worthington sat with her back straight as a ruler. They picked up speed and sailed over a jump made of red and white striped poles, the horse's hooves clearing the top pole with ease. Bill Hesslop and Robbie clapped from their seats on a pile of hay bales.

"Wow! Look at your grandmother!" said Katie as they climbed onto the fence of the corral to watch. "How come she doesn't fall off?"

"Oh, she practices all the time." said Sally. "Grandma says she started riding when she was two. Her Dad put her on a pony and then gave it a spanking. It took off and ran right through some rose bushes and then up those steps in the backyard and into the house. My Dad says grandma is exaggerating about the "into the house" part. He says I get my linguistic flexibility from her. That means I can roll my tongue into funny shapes." Sally stuck her tongue out at Katie and rolled it into a "U" shape.

Katie looked impressed and tried to roll her tongue too, but couldn't quite manage it. She pushed at it with her fingers, but finally gave up. "Your grandmother must be very rich, to live in this big house and have horses and everything. How come you and your Dad and Robbie live in such a small apartment?"

"It's because of the prostate," said Sally, laying Melvin's wet sweater on the top rail of the fence to dry. "My Mom died without a will, so the estate went into Prostate. When it came out all the money stayed with my grandma, cause she's my Mom's mom. Also my Mom and Dad weren't married. They were free spirits. That means they saved lots of money by not getting married. My Dad says that weddings are just huge holes people throw cash into. Which is just stupid. If I had lots of money I wouldn't throw it down a hole. I'd vest it in the sock market. That's what grandma does. My Dad says she's rolling in money. That means she spreads money on the floor and does somersaults on it."

Katie nodded, looking impressed.

Sally waved at her grandmother, who wheeled her horse and trotted over to them.

"Hello, Miss Sally. Would you like to ride Violet here? I've given her a thorough workout, so she's nice and calm."

Bill Hesslop jumped off his hay bale and hurried up to the fence, looking rather alarmed. "I don't think that's such a good idea. Sally, why don't you ride that little pony you were on last time? He's more your speed. He's right over there."

Bill Hesslop pointed to Max, a chubby little Shetland pony who was munching grass in a pasture next to the corral.

"Nonsense, Bill dear," said Mrs. Worthington. "Why, I started riding full-grown horses when I was five. She'll be fine. We'll start slow. Sally dear, come sit up here in front of me."

Mrs. Worthington guided her horse up next to the fence. Sally handed Melvin to Katie and climbed onto the top bar of the fence.

Her grandmother wrapped one arm around Sally's waist and hoisted her into the saddle in front of her. They trotted slowly around the corral, Sally whooping with delight and Bill Hesslop watching nervously. Katie climbed down from the fence and made herself comfortable on a hay bale. She put Melvin on her lap and gave him a good scratch behind the ears. Both of them looked extremely glad they were sitting on a hay bale and not on a horse.

Robbie sat next to them for a while, swinging his chubby legs and chewing on a handful of grass he had yanked up from the pony's pasture, but soon he started to fidget. He climbed down from his hay bale and toddled off toward Max with a determined gleam in his eye. Katie eyed him worriedly, but decided that if she had to choose between watching Melvin and watching Robbie, Melvin was definitely the easier choice.

Max had tired of grass and was ambling over to a pile of sacks bulging with grain which someone had unwisely left in his pasture. With his strong front teeth he tore a hole in one corner of the top sack and a tiny waterfall of grain poured out. As Max indulged himself in this unexpected snack Robbie quietly pulled himself up onto the wobbling pile of grain sacks. He balanced precariously, like a diver on a diving board, then reached out with both hands and awkwardly slid himself stomach first onto the pony's back, where he lay like a very lumpy saddle. Max pulled his nose out of the grain pile in surprise and twisted his head around. He eyed Robbie's rear end curiously, giving a little shake to see if the strange object would fall off. Robbie giggled. Max pricked up his ears at this, deciding this might be a fun game. He started at a slow trot across the pasture. Robbie bounced up and down, laughing hysterically.

Max circled his pasture a few times then headed for the gate, which was closed but not locked. He gave the bars a push with his nose and they were off toward the estate's long gravel drive and freedom.

Behind them footsteps pounded on the gravel. Max sped up, his round belly swaying from side to side. Robbie's giggles got even louder. It looked like the two adventurers were going to pull off their escape into the wide world. But, alas, reality (and a puffing parent) prevailed.

Bill Hesslop ran forward and grabbed Robbie off the pony's back. "That's enough, you two," he said, gasping for air. He set Robbie on his feet and shook his finger at Max. "Max, you should know better. And you, Robbie. With all the dirt and cookies you've managed to tuck away today, all that bouncing is going to make you spew like Old Faithful."

Mrs. Worthington and Sally rode up on Violet. The chestnut mare nickered in a disapproving manner at the pony. Max shook his blond mane at her and began to calmly munch a cluster of dandelions at his feet.

"Oh, I wouldn't worry about our Mr. Robert's digestion," said Mrs. Worthington. "He has a stomach like cast iron. He gets it from his grandpa. That man could eat a five-course Sunday dinner, top if off with three desserts, and then go on the WhirlyGig ride at the State Fair carnival without so much as a twinge of heartburn. Though, I admit he didn't share little Mr. Robert's fondness for soil sampling. You really ought to cure the child of that, Bill dear. I caught him snacking on the compost under my roses the last time he was here. It's a good thing I tell my gardener not to use pesticides."

Bill Hesslop sighed. "Yes, ma'am. I've tried to get Robbie to stop eating dirt. Our doctor says it's just a phase he's going through. He's like a puppy. He'll eat anything. Next he'll probably start chewing on shoes. Well, it's been a pleasure, as always, but we need to get going. I need to get Sally to her school. Her play is tonight and they have one last rehearsal."

"You're coming, right grandma?" said Sally as she slid off of Violet's back. "It's gonna be super terrific. It's about the Pilgrims and the first Thanksgiving. I'm a Squall."

"You mean a Squaw, Sally." said her father.

Sally nodded. "Right. If you're a Naïve American and a girl, then you're a Squall. The boys are Braves, like the baseball team. All the Brownies from my troop are in the play. Course, we don't have boys in the Brownies, so there are some Cub Scouts in the play, but it's still gonna be good."

Mrs. Worthington dismounted. "I'm sure even the Cub Scouts will be unable to dim your thespian brilliance my dear. Of course I'll be there. It will be the highlight of my social season."

End of Excerpt

Made in the USA
Columbia, SC
27 February 2023

13026400R00079